This Is Kind of an EPIC

LOVE STORY

Kheryn Callender

BALZER + BRAY
An Imprint of HarperCollinsPublishers

Balzer + Bray is an imprint of HarperCollins Publishers.

This Is Kind of an Epic Love Story
www.epicreads.com

Library of Congress Cataloging-in-Publication Data
Names: Callender, Kheryn, author.
Title: This is kind of an epic love story / Kheryn Callender.
Description: First edition. | New York, NY : Balzer + Bray, an imprint of
    HarperCollinsPublishers, 2018. | Summary: Budding screenwriter Nate,
    sixteen, finds his conviction that happy endings do not happen in real
    life sorely tested when his childhood best friend and crush, Oliver James
    Hernández, moves back to town.
Identifiers: LCCN 2018005030 | ISBN 9780062820228 (hardback)
Subjects: | CYAC: Best friends—Fiction. | Friendship—Fiction. | High
    schools—Fiction. | Schools—Fiction. | Mothers and sons—Fiction. | Single-
    parent families—Fiction. | Deaf—Fiction. | Bisexuality—Fiction.
Classification: LCC PZ7.1.C317 Thi 2018 | DDC [Fic]—dc23 LC record
available at https://lccn.loc.gov/2018005030

Typography by Michelle Cunningham
18 19 20 21 22   PC/LSCH   10 9 8 7 6 5 4 3 2 1
❖
First Edition

For QPOC everywhere

This Is Kind of an

EPIC
LOVE
STORY

1

RIDING A BIKE IN THE RAIN WITH A BROKEN ARM IS NEVER A good idea, but I'm the kind of guy who likes to make life more difficult, so that's exactly what I do. The rain makes the rubbery brown handles slippery, and it's hard to hold on one-handed, so I end up slowly weaving down the road, wheels jerking back and forth, stopping whenever a car splashes by.

The coffee shop on the corner is one of the many anti-Starbucks bistro spots that've cropped up around Seattle. The inside is a standard hipster café: random Victorian objects hanging on wood-paneled walls, vegan/gluten-free cookies on display, Polaroids hung up around the blackboard menu, probably taken with the old-school camera at the register. Some guy's inspecting the camera now, turning it over and over in his hands and staring at the lens like he wants every-one to know that he's *super into photography*, which I sort of want to judge him for—but I realize judging him is kind of mean and unnecessary, so I stand next to him at the register and pretend I'm not embarrassed to be a sixteen-year-old guy ordering a hot cocoa.

The barista is a cute girl with pale skin and short black hair. She keeps glancing at me and looking away with red cheeks. I should do something. Ask her out. Tell her she looks nice. Wait, is that catcalling? Even if it's inside a hipster café and not out on the street? Fucking shit. I'm a catcalling bastard. She probably doesn't even want to talk to me. Just wants to make a goddamn hot cocoa, and here I come, strolling in and thinking I'm the shit just because a girl smiles at me . . .

"Nate?" she calls, thumping the hot cocoa on the counter.

I stumble up to the counter, mutter a thanks as I reach for the container, but I'm still not used to my arm being in a cast, so I knock the hot chocolate over. It falls, rolls across the counter, and tumbles to the ground. Delicious cocoa and still-melting marshmallows burst on the floor. Everyone turns to look at me. Conversations stop. The cute barista raises an eyebrow. Please kill me now.

The barista—her name tag says *Kim*—gives me a pity smile. "I'll make you another one?" she says with a shrug.

I force a laugh, but it sounds more like a cough. "Uh. That's really nice. Thanks."

Conversations start up again, people glancing over. I try to act cool, bend over with a handful of those thin, square napkins to clean up the mess, but the napkins get soggy and start to fall apart instantly. Someone else bends over with more of them bunched up in his hand. It's the guy who was fiddling with the camera, which makes me feel like an asshole for judging him, when he's clearly a nice person. He's got brown hair tumbling into his face, brown eyes that shine with the kindness of a thousand nuns, the kind of dimples that'd make even a coldhearted soul want to pinch his cheeks. I would know, because that's kind of what I want to do. He smiles at me as he sops up the mess.

"Thanks," I tell him. He shakes his head, looks away, still smiling—not a big deal. I keep glancing up at him. I can't place it, but he's really familiar. I feel like I've seen him in a TV commercial, or a movie, or on a poster for ridiculously adorable guys, or—

He gets up and tosses his napkins in the trash. I thank him again, but he ignores me as he walks out, the bell on the door ringing as it shuts behind him. I pick up my second hot chocolate, staring after him.

It's only when I'm unlocking my rusted blue bike outside, fumbling with the combination, that it hits me.

I know exactly who he is.

Oliver James Hernández.

Holy fucking shit.

* * *

The rain is more like a mist. It slicks the leaves and green covering the barks of trees and shines on the granite road so that it looks like black glass. When I finally get to Florence's, I'm soaked. Flo opens the door, takes one look at me, and bursts out laughing.

"What happened to you? Why're you so wet?"

I stare at her blankly. "It's raining."

She glances past me. "Eh. It's more like mist."

I abandon the bicycle on her doorstep and step inside, kicking off my sneakers, holding out the hot cocoa for her, hoping to God her dad isn't here, because Florence's dad has never liked me very much. Tobey Maguire, her black dachshund, wiggles over and licks my foot before he starts humping it.

"Really? That's all the foreplay I get?"

"Tobey!" Florence picks him up. "I swear to God, Tobey, I'm going to cut off your balls."

I wince. "Don't cut his balls off."

Florence grins at me. "Sympathy pains?"

"It's not funny."

"It's a little funny."

"No. No, it really isn't."

She carries Tobey up the stairs, cradling him like a baby, chugging the hot chocolate like it's iced tea. The TV is off, and I don't hear any voices from the living room, so I can safely

4

say that Florence and I are alone in the house. The thought makes me think things I probably shouldn't—not anymore, anyway.

We get into her room, which smells like baby powder, and she closes the door behind me, hopping and bouncing onto her flowery bed. Ethel, her evil cat from hell, is curled up on one of the lacy pillows, blinking at me slowly. There're clumps of dirty clothes around the floor, and Flo's desk has this year's new textbooks stacked up and a worn copy of a Neil Gaiman comic open like a tent. Her laptop, screen dusty and smeared, streams the Bon Iver Pandora station.

I almost tell her about the café—about seeing who was either Oliver James for the first time in five years, or his equally attractive doppelgänger—but I don't even know where to start. How do I begin to explain Oliver James Hernández?

Flo doesn't notice my silent struggle, but I can't blame her, because I'm pretty good at hiding inner turmoil when I want to. She pats the side of the bed with a *come hither* look on her face, ink pen between her fingers. I sit down and hold my arm out, and she begins to draw. The design on my cast is made up of characters from my favorite films. Buttercup and Westley gazing into each other's eyes, Olive Hoover with her arms spread wide, Joel Barish lying down beside Clementine Kruczynski, Juno and Paulie singing to each other on the front steps. Florence sticks out the tip of her tongue in concentration. I have to look away, or I'll end up remembering the days when her dad wasn't home and I'd come over and that tongue would be soft and wet against mine, and we'd make Tobey Maguire proud with our best dry-humping techniques, legs and hands and mouths all tangled together in a pile of horniness—and then, before we could hit the place of no return, I always stopped. Said that we should wait. Florence joked in the mostly serious kind of way that I was the only guy she knew that would ever willingly not have sex.

Florence is black and Taiwanese and has brown skin, almost as dark as mine, with twists she dyed a dark purple. They're tied into a bun on top of her head, some twists falling down around her ears and into her face, which she swipes away impatiently. She isn't wearing a bra, only has on a thin white T-shirt, so I can pretty much see an outline of what's beneath if I look, but I try not to. I really do.

"Lydia's being an ass," Florence says. She glances at me over the rims of her glasses, and I look up at her with an expression of innocence, as if I wasn't staring at her breasts like the creeper I am. "It's like she's purposely picking fights with me now."

"Oh." I'm not really sure if this is the sort of thing Flo and I should be talking about.

She glances up from my cast like she's read my mind. "You know, it's okay if you don't want to talk about her. I mean, I get it."

I don't want to talk about Lydia. But Flo's also my friend,

and friends talk to friends about their love lives, right? "No—uh, it's okay." I clear my throat. "Do you want to break up with her?"

"No. Does that make me pathetic?"

"Why would it make you pathetic?"

"Because I'm chasing after someone who's treating me like shit."

"That doesn't make you pathetic. That makes you just like everyone else. Human."

She sighs and leans in closer to my arm, her shirt gaping open so that I actually can see what's going on beneath. Christ. I close my eyes.

"I don't know," she says. "Maybe she isn't really being an ass. Maybe I'm overreacting. I mean, she's stressing out because of her parents and everything—she's getting all this pressure to get into RISD. I should just be supportive. She's always supportive of me when I'm going through shit."

I feel a pinch of jealousy that I try to ignore. It isn't fair to Florence. Thinking these things, feeling this way. A few months back, we agreed we weren't good together as a couple. I was getting too codependent, too clingy and self-conscious. Flo was pushing me away, started hanging out with Lydia more—until one night she came over, saying that they'd made out, crying because she felt like shit about it, telling me she didn't want us to date anymore. *You're right*, I'd told her. *I think we should go back to being friends, too.* I knew it was a lie then. I know it's a lie now.

Florence scratches away at my cast with her pen and falls into a silence that lets me know that she's in the zone. I try to hold extra still. José González streams from her laptop. The bed shifts, and I look at her just as she drops her hand.

She smiles. "It's done."

I try to twist my arm around, but there's a stab of pain that makes my fingers tingle. Florence grabs her phone and turns it to self-view on her camera for me. There's Tina, tied up to her pole. I can't help but grin. I love it. "Thanks, Flo."

She scoops up Tobey and plays with his floppy ears. I should go. It isn't really late, but the first day of school starts tomorrow, and it won't be easy to wake up in the morning after spending the last two months sleeping until noon, watching and re-watching movies on Netflix until I feel brave enough to attempt writing one of my many scripts again.

Florence smiles at me as she scratches Tobey behind his ears. I know that smile. Nothing good can come of that smile. "What about you?" she asks with a too-innocent voice.

I look at her, question mark on my face.

"When're you going to find someone new?"

My neck gets a little warm, and it's hard to speak. "Uh. I don't know."

She groans. "Oh, come *on*, Bird."

I feel myself getting a little defensive. "What? Not everyone needs to be in a relationship. I'm confident enough in who I am to not be in a relationship."

"Yeah, but you're a junior and you're still a virgin," she says with a wince.

I pause. "I'm happy being a virgin."

"Oh, please. No one's happy being a virgin."

"I mean. Some people are happy being a virgin."

"Right, but are you really one of them?"

I hesitate.

"That's what I thought." She scratches Tobey's ears. "We could always get back together again," she says, not looking at me. "I wouldn't mind defiling you."

I laugh. "You make it sound so dirty."

She just keeps her small smile. It makes me wonder. Wonder if maybe she's been thinking things about me, same things that I've been thinking about her. I can't help it. I automatically start to feel all tingly and warm. I have to remind myself: Florence broke up with me for a reason. I know she doesn't feel that way about me anymore. Because she told me. In those exact words. "*I'm sorry, Nate. I just don't feel that way about you anymore.*" I'm lucky we could stay friends. I don't want to ruin that by obsessing over her. I just have to accept our unhappy ending.

I loved movies with happy endings when I was a kid. I mean, who doesn't? The mushy, feel-good dialogue where everyone knows how to say exactly the right thing at exactly the right time, the warmth you get knowing that, for this one moment, happiness has found a way to be immortalized, the sunsets. Everyone loves a happy ending with a good sunset.

But I eventually figured it out. Happy endings aren't real.

American Beauty.

The Departed.

Melancholia.

Memento.

They've got it right.

The *Notting Hill* and *You've Got Mail* and *Sixteen Candles* movies of the world have people thinking that life is an endless series of well-placed jokes and three acts where even the most fucked-up humans in the world can find redemption and love. It's just not true.

Don't get me wrong. I still love watching movies with a good happy ending. They're a flicker of light in an otherwise depressing-as-fuck world. But is it realistic?

Nope. No, not really.

My arm is starting to ache. Five more weeks and the cast comes off. I get to my feet and start toward the door, but stop when I notice Florence hasn't gotten up to walk me downstairs. She's watching me carefully, squinting behind her cat-eye glasses.

"You're over me," she says, "right?"

Crap. I hesitate, blink too fast. "Yeah, I'm over you," I say.

A moment of uncomfortable silence. Seriously, I'm the king of awkward. I just try to embrace it.

"We'll find you someone else," she says confidently. "By the end of the year, you'll be a virgin no more. Let's bring it in."

"Oh, come on, Flo—"

She gives me a scary look. She reminds me of Ethel a little too much sometimes.

I hold out my good hand and she puts hers on top of mine.

"Clear eyes. Full hearts. Can't lose."

She kisses my cheek and leads me to the door.

It's stopped misting outside, and I decide to walk my bike instead, but walking a bike with only one good arm is just as impossible as riding it, so it almost takes an hour to get home. The sun's basically down by then, making the sky the shadowed sort of blue-green before night comes. Fresh after-rain and pine scent fills the air. I pass the house at the top of the hill, the one that always has my heart beating a little harder and my palms getting gross-sweaty as I'm bombarded by memories I'd much rather forget. Tonight I see there's a moving van out front with some soggy boxes on the sidewalk. It can't just be a coincidence, right? Oliver James is definitely back.

I almost consider hiding behind a tree to see if he'll come outside or not, but I realize that'd officially make me a stalker, so I hurry down the hill to my house and leave the bike propped up against the garage wall before I unlock the front door and step inside. All the lights are off. The house has been a little depressing ever since Rebecca went to Chicago a few weeks back, so these days I usually just go straight to my bedroom and stay there—but before I can get out of the foyer, my mom calls my name. I hold in a sigh and cross over to the living room. She's curled up on the sofa under a blanket. Another rerun of *Friends* is on TV.

She smiles, sits up. "Were you visiting Florence?"

"Yep."

"How's she doing?"

I shrug. "I don't know. Good, I guess." I don't like talking about Flo with my mom. She's forever asking why we broke up, saying that we were *so cute* together, like we were puppies behind a glass window in a pet store—but I'm guessing she wouldn't think it's very cute that Flo cheated on me, so I just try to avoid the topic altogether now.

Her smile falters and she nods. "Well, you cut it a little close tonight," she says, picking up her cell phone and flashing the screen at me: 6:54 p.m.

"About that," I say, clearing my throat and standing a little straighter. "I'm sixteen, and as of tomorrow, I'm officially a junior."

She crosses her arms. "Go on. . . ."

"I—uh—think it's time that my curfew comes to an end."

Her smile fades completely. "We've talked about this, Nate."

"Come on," I say, crossing the room and leaning on the

back of the couch. "No one else in my grade has a *seven o'clock* curfew. I mean, ten, maybe—"

"No one else in your grade has me for a mother," she says with a pearly smile.

"Yep. That's very true."

"I would just feel better knowing that you're home, safely watching Netflix and whatever else it is that teen boys do in their rooms—"

I smack a hand to my face. "God, Mom."

She ignores me. "Besides, as you said, it's your junior year. This is the time to be focusing on your homework, your exams, getting the best grades that you can. You shouldn't be out gallivanting at all hours of the night."

"Gallivanting?" I say. "Hanging out with Flo isn't gallivanting. We literally just sit around and talk and watch movies."

"If you want to get into a good college," she continues, "you'll need to work hard this year. Seattle University isn't exactly a cakewalk, you know."

She always acts like I have no choice but to go to a college in the area—and the scary part is that I'm pretty sure she's being 100 percent serious. "I'm going to bed," I say.

"Good life choice," she says, tapping her cheek. I roll my eyes and kiss it as super quickly as I can before turning to leave, and hold in a sigh as she adds, "Maybe I should apply to Seattle University, too—I've always wanted a second degree."

"Good night, Mom," I say over my shoulder.

I can hear the laughter in her voice. "Good night, Nate."

I run up the stairs and into my bedroom, lean against the door and shut my eyes. I know I should go downstairs and try to stop being such a shitty son and spend time with my mom—especially tonight. The first day of school is usually around the anniversary of when my dad died, and this year, it's tomorrow. September 5. I was only nine when it happened—but sometimes I'll walk by the spot where the Ridgemont movie theater used to be, or I'll see some stranger from the back and for a split second think it's him, and it'll feel like it just happened all over again.

I remember Mom trying not to cry as she sat me and Becca down in the living room. She started telling us that there'd been an accident, but she couldn't finish. She broke down sobbing. Becca didn't even understand what happened yet, but she still got up and hugged our mom and said it was going to be okay, which made our mom cry even harder.

I didn't know what to do. I just sat there and watched, feeling completely helpless. I guess that's kind of what I'm still doing, even seven years later.

It's been hard for me, growing up without my dad, mostly because I wonder how I might be different now if I had him around. Would he have made me a better person somehow? Maybe I wouldn't have been so clingy with Florence. Maybe we'd still be together, and my dad would have to give me some embarrassing talk about being safe. It's the not knowing what

I've missed out on that hurts almost as much as the pain of losing him does.

But it must be even worse for my mom. I can't imagine what it's like, losing the love of your life. I can't go down there, can't face her pain. I don't know what to say to comfort her, so I'm too afraid to say anything at all.

2

THE LAST DAY OF SUMMER VACATION IS EXCITING IN A nerve-racking way, but it can be a little depressing, too, and not just because school is about to begin again (though I guess that's about 85 percent of the reason), but because I start questioning the kind of person I want to be this year, and it makes me wonder—I mean, if I have to question it, maybe I don't even know who I really am.

My phone buzzes in my pocket, and I see a text from my sister.

Love you, Nate. Be extra nice to mom today. XOXO

It's the first time we're not spending the anniversary together. Usually our mom would take us to the cemetery in the morning, and we'd put fresh flowers on my dad's gravestone before heading to school—but today my mom's bedroom door was closed, and I'm pretty sure I could hear her crying, so I stood outside her door for a minute, unsure of what to do, before I finally left.

I suck at texting, so I pocket my phone as I walk through the parking lot that smells like a mixture between burning oil and fresh pine needles. I look up to see a rusted red car right in front of me—and Florence and Lydia leaning against it. Lydia doesn't even go to Ballard. She attends some fancy private arts school down in Bellevue. She must've driven Florence here to make it up to her after their latest fight.

Lydia sees me. We make a silent agreement not to say hello. I try to take a quick left, but I can see Florence's head turning in the corner of my eye.

"Bird!" she calls.

I wish I had my earbuds in—then I could pretend I hadn't heard her. I take a deep breath and turn, plastering on a grin and walking over.

"Hey." I put up my good hand, the other stuffed in my hoodie's pocket.

Florence's smile wavers. It looks like she didn't think past calling my name. She desperately wants me and Lydia to be friends, but that probably won't happen any time soon, seeing that whenever the three of us are together, there's nothing but awkward silence.

Lydia always looks like she's too self-assured (or maybe too full of herself) to feel uncomfortable, so she doesn't bother trying to come up with a conversation topic. Her hair's dyed a fiery red, her brown skin glows, she's got a septum and a lip piercing, and she wears a Nirvana T-shirt, cut-off black shorts, and black combat boots. Translation: she's much cooler than I'll ever be.

I decide to try—for Florence's sake. "How was your summer?" I ask her.

She looks me over like she can't believe this is the best I could come up with. "Fine," she says shortly. She turns and kisses Florence's cheek. "I have to go, babe, or I'll be late."

Florence bites her lip, glancing at me. "Okay."

I hold in a sigh and start walking away, giving them some privacy, though the kissing sounds follow me. I think I might be sick. I'm still walking when Florence jogs to catch up to me and Lydia speeds by, blaring her horn.

"Nice of her to drive you," I say.

She smiles a little. "Yeah. You know, I was thinking—maybe we should try hanging out again soon. Just to get past all the awkwardness. I really think you two would like each other."

I really don't think we would, but I don't want to say that to Flo. We pass through the parking lot and down the tree-lined path toward the courtyard filled with wooden benches, where people usually eat lunch and hang out, and where the nicer teachers bring their classes when it isn't raining. Florence sits down on her favorite bench, still damp from an early rain shower. She's got on baggy pants and a tank top and bangles that go up and down her arms. I feel plain and boring next to her, in the thin hipster jeans and hoodies and Converses that make up my entire wardrobe. She hooks her arm with my good one when I sit down beside her.

"How're you doing?" she asks. She knows about the anniversary.

I shrug, because I don't really know how to talk about it. "I'm okay. I'm just worried about my mom, I guess."

She gives me a sympathetic nod. "Yeah."

We sit there together, watching the trail of students fill up the courtyard, hugging and laughing and taking selfies. Ballard has its groups of friends, and yeah, there are assholes here like anywhere else, but it's not like *Mean Girls* with everyone sitting in their assigned cafeteria seats.

"There's something so depressing about the first day of school," Florence says.

This is why I love her. She gets it without me having to say a single word.

"Maybe we should just ditch."

She gives me an appalled look. "Skip school on the first day? When did you become such a rebel?"

I try not to laugh. "I've always been a rebel. You just never noticed."

Her smile falters. We've now entered the dangerous territory of flirtation.

She recovers with a grin. "So, Bird," she starts, "who's

going to be the lucky soul to help you lose your virginity?"

I swing my head around. "Say that a little louder, would you?"

"It's nothing to be ashamed of," she says, and actually seems serious. "But it's definitely not going to happen if you just sit around *wishing* you could have sex."

"Why're you so obsessed with my love life?" I ask her, only half joking—but there's a flicker of hurt in her eyes.

She shrugs, unhooks from my arm to cross her own. "Just trying to help." A familiar shadow of guilt crosses her face. She tore my heart up into little pieces when she cheated on me, and she knows it. "It's the least I can do, I guess."

These are the moments that still have my heart beating a little too hard for her. "You can't keep blaming yourself."

"For sticking my tongue down someone else's throat?" she says with a small smile. "Of course I can."

I rub the back of my neck. "Everyone makes mistakes, right?"

"Yeah, but I really fucked up with that one." She glances at me. "I'm lucky we could stay friends." And she puts her hand on top of mine, clenching my fingers. Probably because she doesn't realize I'm still in love with her.

My smile feels strained. "Yeah. I'm lucky too."

The bell rings, and there's that awkward moment where we don't know how much longer to hold hands, until Flo just laughs and kisses me on the cheek, which I already know is going to be the best thing that'll happen to me today. We're standing up to go inside, but across the courtyard of benches I see Ashley Perkins talking to someone. Someone with a tangle of curly hair and bright brown eyes and dimples I can see from here, probably could see from across a soccer field.

Florence follows my gaze and misinterprets my surprised expression. "New kid is cute," she says. Elbows my side. "Is this a potential candidate for Project: Nate Loses His Virginity?"

I can't even breathe. "No, he's not a *candidate*. Jesus."

Flo tugs the end of my hoodie. "Come on, let's go introduce ourselves."

"No—wait—Florence. *Florence.*" But she's already up and walking away (her butt looks really great in those pants, not that I'm staring at her butt *at all*). She turns to beam at me before she crosses to Ashley and Oliver James. It'd be a thousand times worse if I just sat here, so I force myself to my feet and cross the courtyard too.

I do an awkward wave as I reach them. Oliver James wears an oversized sweater, jeans with holes around the knees, and sneakers. His cheeks are a little blotchy from the chill in the air, and some curls fall into his eyes. Ollie was always a pretty serious kid, and now he looks like a pretty serious guy—like it'd take a lot to make him smile. A real smile, not just one that's polite. He's always given me the feeling that when he looks at me, he's trying to take everything in at once. Like he's trying to get a read on who I am and everything I want with one glance.

He looks at me with all that weight in his gaze. I don't think he recognizes me. I can't exactly blame him. It's been five years, and my kid photos look like they belong to some weird second cousin.

"Hey." I'm not sure what to say. How do I make this situation *not* awkward? *Hi there, Ollie—remember me? It's Nate, your former best friend, before I fucked everything up.* "Uh—Oliver, right?"

Ashley looks between the two of us, surprised. "Oh—do you already know Nate?" She pulls out her phone, types, and hands it to him.

Oliver James reads the message, gives the phone back to her. "I know him," he says, and his tone is different, with a bit of an accent. "It's been a few years."

Florence raises an eyebrow.

Ollie watches me, waiting for me to speak, and it couldn't be more obvious that he'd rather be anywhere else in the universe than standing beside me.

I clear my throat. "Yeah. Five years. Well, more like four years and a few months. A long time, I guess. I didn't expect you to come back. I mean, I didn't think I'd ever see you again—"

The bell rings. Thank God.

Ashley taps Oliver's shoulder. "Do you want help finding your class?"

Oliver nods. "That'd be great. Thank you."

The two walk off arm in arm, leaving me and Florence behind. I don't look at her, but I can feel her stare.

"You know Cute New Guy, and you didn't say anything?"

"I tried to tell you."

"Okay," she says slowly. "And what, exactly, is the deal between you two?"

That's something I hope I'll never have to explain. "Come on, we'll be late for homeroom."

3

I SPEND MOST OF THE DAY RACING FROM CLASS TO CLASS, peering over my shoulder and acting like a level-10 freak whenever I see anyone with brown curls. Luckily, I haven't had any classes with Oliver for the morning—I can't imagine sitting at a desk, trying not to look at Oliver James, but totally aware of him, like a miniature sun burning in the corner of my eye.

But he's sitting right up front in biology. Ashley stands next to him, loudly telling him about different teachers and classes—she has a thing about trying to help new students. I see Ollie, pretend I don't see him, and head straight for the back of the room. Florence sits down in the desk next to mine with a *what the fuck is wrong with you?* expression.

Gideon slides into the desk on my other side. People used to call him Weasley to make fun of him. He's white and tall and skinny as hell and has the red hair, the pale face, even the freckles. But then last year, his skinniness became more lean, and he was elected class president and became the captain of the soccer team and even starred in the school play. Half the school started flocking to him. He still hangs with me and Flo and Ashley, talking movies with me and comics with Florence and playing video games with Ashley, but he's also got a bit of a Kanye West vibe to him now.

He nods his head at Ashley and Ollie. "Who's Ash talking to?"

I pull out my notebook and slap it on the desk. "Oliver James Hernández. He used to live here. Just moved back."

"I don't like him. Five minutes and he's already got everyone giggling and whispering."

And I mean, yeah, I guess Ollie's getting a couple of curious glances, but more in the new-kid way than anything else. "Ashley's the only person even looking at him."

Gideon watches like he isn't the least bit concerned to be caught staring. "He's just over there, soaking it all up."

I roll my eyes. "I wouldn't say he's *soaking it up*." Just as I say it, I notice Ollie watching. His eyes widen and we both look away. So, so awkward.

Gideon notices the exchange. "What, you know him?"

"We used to be friends," I say, then regret it—I can tell

Florence is listening, even if her eyes are on the sketches in her notebook.

Gideon narrows his eyes at me, like he's trying to figure out what *used to* means, but before he can ask any questions, the teacher walks in with an interpreter, who waves at Ollie and walks over to his desk to begin signing.

Ashley hurries down the aisle, tripping over a backpack and saying, "Sorry, sorry, sorry" before she finally makes it to her seat beside Gideon, breathless. "Ollie's so freaking cute. I just want to put him in my pocket and take him home."

Gideon rolls his eyes. "It's only the first day, and you already have an insta-crush?"

Flo lets out a loud sigh. "Ignore him. He's just being dramatic because he's afraid people will think Ollie's hotter than he is."

"But Ollie's adorable," Ash says. "It doesn't mean I have an *insta-crush* on him. It's just a fact. He's cute."

Gideon groans. "No—no, he effing isn't."

Florence peers at Gideon skeptically over the rims of her glasses. Gideon looks at me, like he's waiting for me to agree.

I almost refuse to answer. Just silently return his stare. I mean, come on—it's ridiculous, arguing over whether Oliver's cute or not. But entering a staring match with Gideon is never a good idea. He'll just keep watching me expectantly until the school day ends. Even from across the hallways and in the middle of class, he'll make a point to swing his head and keep staring.

I shrug. "I don't know—I mean, yeah, I guess he's good-looking." I say that partly to piss Gideon off. And partly because it's true.

Ashley bites her lip, glancing at Gideon. "I kind of want to ask him out."

Florence exchanges a weird look with me. "Really?" she says.

It's pretty much gone unsaid, but we always assumed Ashley had a crush on Gideon. Sure, half the school does too—but she liked him before it was a trend. They've always been friends. While Flo and I are hanging out and watching Netflix, the two of them are over at Ashley's place, playing *Overwatch* or *Halo* together. But recently, Ash has also started to laugh just a little more loudly at all of Gideon's jokes, and stares at him when she doesn't think anyone else is watching, and well, I just figured it was only a matter of time before they started going out.

If Gideon ever shows a sign that he's interested also, anyway.

Gideon flips his phone onto his desk. "What happened to not having an insta-crush on him?"

Ash sits on the edge of her seat, playing with the ends of her curled brown hair. She somehow looks like Selena Gomez and Vanessa Hudgens and Jenna Coleman combined. "I don't have a crush on him. I've only known him for, like, five minutes. But I'd like to get to know him so that I could, possibly, maybe . . ."

The teacher begins scratching chalk across the board. Flo lowers her voice. "You just never really struck me as the dating type, is all."

Ashley narrows her eyes at Florence. "What's that supposed to mean?" We get a few over-the-shoulder glances, and Ash sinks herself lower in her seat.

Flo shrugs. "I mean—you just—"

"You're either at school, hanging out with us, or playing video games," Gideon says.

Ashley's cheeks get pink. "So what?"

Flo says, a little more gently, "So we just assumed you weren't interested." She looks at me, and I can practically read her mind: *Interested in anyone but Gideon, anyway.*

"You shouldn't make assumptions about people, Florence," Ashley says under her breath. We're all quiet for another second, before Ash adds, "I'm sixteen, and I've never been in a relationship before. It's time to try new things."

Gideon taps the edge of his desk with his pencil. "Oh, I'm sure you can try a *lot* of new things with Oliver James Hernández."

Ashley hides her face in her hands. Florence tells him to stop being an asshole.

"Why am I being an asshole?"

"You know you're being an asshole."

"No, I don't actually know that—"

Ashley interrupts. "I'm not a virgin."

We all swing our heads to look at Ashley. Gideon's brows are up in his hairline. Ash pretends not to notice and studiously takes out her notebook and pen. When we don't look away, she whispers, "What? It's not a big deal."

We all turn back to the front of the class.

Now I'm pretty sure all of my friends have already done the dirty. Florence definitely has (I've heard just a few too many details about her escapades with Lydia), and Gideon's hooked up with just about every girl who's thrown herself at him. And now, even Ashley—Ash, who I was pretty sure hadn't even kissed anyone before—has done the deed.

I get that for a lot of people, it's not something to hesitate over—all the TV shows and movies with horny-as-fuck guys jumping at any opportunity to have sex for the first time makes me feel like I'm a freak for saying no . . . but that just wasn't me. Yeah, I wanted to have sex with Florence—but a bigger part of me wanted to wait. Make sure we were both ready. I'd told Flo I wasn't ready, because I was scared sex would change how we felt about each other, or I'd mess up everything between us—but I guess I don't even really know what *being ready* means. "*I'm not ready, Flo. We have to make sure that we're both ready.*" Shit. I could effing kick myself.

The morning is a blur of reunions and introductions. Oliver James isn't in any other class with me, thank God. Teachers lecture us to be the best students we can be, and tell us that the choices we make this year can pave the roads we take for the rest of our lives. Which is, you know. No pressure at all.

Rebecca already helped me check out some colleges with screenwriting programs. None of the ones I like are here in Seattle. I'm not sure how my mom's going to take that. I can feel her grip tightening. Can feel her realizing I'm going to leave when I graduate. She doesn't want me to go. She doesn't want to be alone. The guilt of wanting to leave might kill me before I actually do.

Lunch starts and I end up in the greenhouse that smells like wet dirt and fertilizer with its blooming flowers and Jurassic-looking plants and benches that're supposed to be used for class. It's where I've eaten lunch with Flo, Ash, and Gideon since we were freshmen. Flo thinks most of our classmates are a pain in the ass, and most people think Ash is a little annoying, so she usually only hangs around us. I'm not great with meeting and hanging out with dozens of people. Gideon sometimes sits with other groups, since he's basically friends with everyone in the entire school now, but I'm not like that. If I can have a few close friends that I really connect with, that's all I need.

Ashley is in a heated argument with Gideon over which *Dragon Age* is the best ("*Origins* was ahead of its time! It's unfair to say it isn't the best because the graphics aren't as good as *Inquisition*," she says). Florence flips through a *Black*

Panther comic, José González streaming from her phone. My heart drops. Oliver James is there too. He sits a little straighter on the bench when I walk in. I try to force a smile, but too late—of course he sees my expression.

He watches me with that heavy gaze. "Hope you don't mind if I join?" he says.

I hesitate. Flo speaks up for me. "Of course he doesn't mind."

She gives me a pointed look and pats an empty seat that just happens to be right across from Oliver. Ollie is quiet, leg bouncing up and down as he glances up at me and looks away. He cracks his knuckles—a bad old habit that started around the time he began to learn sign language.

When we were ten, he got really sick. It wasn't until I was older that I realized how serious meningitis is—how he could've died. He was stuck in bed for months, in and out of the hospital. He lost his hearing—completely in his right ear and almost all of it in his left, though he can hear a low level of sound, so he can sometimes tell when someone is speaking, though he doesn't understand what they're saying.

When he got better, Ollie's parents got him a private tutor so that he could learn ASL. He'd teach me new words every day. We were friends before, but having that purpose, that mission, to figure out how to communicate with each other again—it brought us closer.

It's funny. We have this whole history, an entire story that's just ours, but we can't even look at each other now.

"Why does the school have a greenhouse?" he asks Ashley.

Flo leans in front of Ashley. "Oh, don't you know?" Florence asks before Ash can say anything. "Our campus is secretly Hogwarts."

Ollie squints at her. "What?"

"Oh, wait." Florence pulls out her phone, types, and shows him the screen. He reads it and laughs—a real one: eyes lighting up, dimples shining. I feel a spark of jealousy.

Ashley taps Oliver's arm to get his attention, handing him her phone. "We have an environmental program. Some nearby colleges even use it on the weekends."

"That's cool," Oliver says, giving hers back. "But I think I like the idea of Hogwarts better."

"Oh, let me guess," Flo says, waving her hand at him. "Hufflepuff?"

He shakes his head, grinning.

"Oh, he's a total Gryffindor," I say before I can stop myself. Ollie hasn't seen me speaking, but everyone gives me a surprised glance. "I mean—at least, he was. When we were kids." I'm just going to shut up now.

"Gryffindor, huh?" Flo says, like she's impressed.

Oliver James shakes his head. "What'd you say?"

"Nothing," Florence says, speaking more loudly, which makes me want to facepalm. She points at me. "It's just that Nate said you're a Gryffindor."

Ollie shakes his head again, not understanding, and tries

to wave his hand at Flo to get her to drop it and move on—he always got frustrated and embarrassed when conversations stopped because he couldn't understand—but Florence only grins at him like it isn't a big deal and pulls out her phone to type. Oliver's eyebrow flicks up as he glances at me. I really wish I hadn't said anything.

Gideon says that he's a Gryffindor, and Flo and Ashley both say, "No you're not, Hufflepuff," which starts Gideon on a rant about how one quiz taken an entire year ago can't determine his Hogwarts house for the rest of his life. No one's really paying attention to me and Oliver James. Oliver glances my way again.

I rub the back of my neck. "Uh. I guess you moved back in the same house on top of the hill?"

He frowns a little. "Sorry, I haven't had to lip-read so much for a while. It's kind of exhausting." I know hanging around a group of hearing people can be annoying for him, too.

"Don't be sorry." I pull out my phone and type my question.

Without looking up from the phone, he makes the sign for "yes," fist knocking down, before he starts signing at warp speed, hands moving way too fast for me. He pauses, realizes he's signing even though I'm hearing—but we used to sign to each other all the time when we were kids. We liked that no one else around could understand us.

He opens his mouth to speak, but I wave my hand,

interrupting him. "It's okay to keep signing. If you want to, anyway."

He hesitates, then signs more slowly. He shakes his head, letting his thumb flick the underside of his chin, raises both hands and beckons with his fingers upside down. The house didn't sell. His fingers hesitate before he keeps going, but I only understand when he raises his hand, palm flat, letting his thumb press into his chin, and when his index finger taps the right side of his chest twice and crosses to the left. *Mom* and *we*.

"You moved back to the same house with your mom?"

He nods.

"I didn't realize you knew sign language," Florence says, the others watching us now. I guess my best friend should know if I understand a second language, but it never came up—and I wasn't about to mention Oliver James. Besides, I'm nowhere near fluent, and without years of practice, I've forgotten most of what Ollie taught me. Probably because I wanted to forget about Ollie himself.

Florence is sitting close enough for Oliver James to read what she said. "He learned a little when we were kids, since he hung around me so much," Ollie offers when it's clear I have no intention of speaking.

Gideon's squinting his eyes at me. "You said you two used to be friends, right?"

Oliver's going to let me take this one. I shrug. "Yeah, before he moved away." Which is a pretty watered-down version of what happened, but I sure as hell am not going to give more details than that.

A silence stretches on. It's pretty effing awkward. *Everyone* knows that something happened between the two of us, but no one wants to ask about it—and Oliver James and I clearly aren't about to admit to anything.

"How're classes going?" Florence asks Ollie, breaking the horrible tension.

Oliver shrugs, says aloud, "They're all right. The school's providing an interpreter and notes from lesson plans and everything."

Ashley sits at the edge of her seat. "I can also give you notes for biology, if you need them."

Ollie doesn't see her speaking. "And I got into photography class, even though it's for seniors. I was a little worried my art credits wouldn't transfer over and I'd have to take another elective."

"That's great," Ash says, leaning forward, clearly trying to smile in a way that is meant to be flirty, though it really just comes across as uncomfortable for everyone involved. Flo makes a gagging noise in my ear. "Is there anyone that you think is cute?" Ashley asks, not wasting any more time. When she sets her mind to something, she really goes for it.

All eyes turn to Ollie. He hesitates. "Did you ask me if I think someone's cute?"

Ashley nods, still smiling.

"Before you answer that, I think you should know,"

Gideon says, leaning across the bench to look at him, "that everyone wants to put you in their pockets."

We groan. Flo tells Gideon to shut up. Ollie looks to me, confused, like maybe he didn't see Gideon's mouth properly. I don't want to tell him what Gideon said, though, so I pause—and with me and Flo and Ash making faces, without really knowing if it was something he did or something someone else said, and all eyes on him . . . Ollie's face turns red.

"What's it like," Gideon asks over the groans, "being the guy everyone wants to sex up?"

"Gideon, for the love of God, shut the hell up," Florence says.

"What? It's true, right? Everyone thinks he's cute. Even Bird said it. That's not a bad thing."

Oliver looks like he wants nothing more than to curl up in a corner and die, and now, I'm pretty sure I'd like to join him. *Even Bird said it.* What the hell is that?

"Why're you being such an asshole?" Flo demands.

"No—you know, you're right. I'm sorry," Gideon says, leaning over the bench table to give Ollie full view of his face. "To be honest, I'm just jealous because everyone has insta-crushes on you."

Ollie lets out a small laugh. Ashley rolls her eyes. But the air is cleared. Tension gone, for the most part. Oliver and I glance at each other again.

"I—uh—actually have a boyfriend," he says. "Back in Santa Fe."

My eyebrows skyrocket.

"Oh," Ash says, disappointed. "That's nice."

"Yeah," Ollie says. "His name's Aiden. We're trying the long-distance thing."

I'm quiet. I think I might be a little disappointed, too.

"Oh, I know," Florence says to Ollie. "You should come with us to film club."

No. Florence. What the hell are you doing?

"Film club?" he says.

"It's nothing crazy," she adds. "We literally just watch movies. It'll be fun."

Oliver looks at me across the bench, like he's waiting for my permission. A part of me wants nothing more than to say no, he can't come—as if I have some sort of ownership over film club, my sacred space from everything that's wrong with the world.

"Yeah," I say. "You should come."

Ollie smiles a little. It's the realest smile he's given me all day. It has my heart thumping just a little harder. "Okay. Yeah, I'd like that."

When the bell rings, Ashley grabs my elbow and drags me to the side, away from the table, where everyone's packing up to go to class. "You guys used to be best friends, right?" she asks, eyes flitting to Oliver James.

I'm not even sure I want to answer. Nothing good can come of this. "Yeah," I say, then decide to add, "about five years ago."

She ignores the "five years ago" part. "Can you talk to him for me?" When I make a face, she adds, "Just ask him if he's interested in me. That's all you have to do."

"Ash, you heard what he said—"

"Yeah, that he has a boyfriend," she says. "That doesn't mean anything. People can have more than one partner. Maybe he's in an open relationship." I don't think I've ever seen Ashley this determined. Maybe even a little desperate.

I cross my arms. "Why do you want to go out with him so badly?"

She shrugs, but her cheeks turn pink. "To prove to myself that I can, I guess. Everyone else already knows me from when we were kids, and no one thinks of me that way, but Oliver James . . ." She rolls her eyes at herself. "Please, just see if he's interested. It's not a big deal to ask him for me, right?"

I clench my jaw. Ash and I weren't always friends. In freshman year, she was the girl who always raised her hand in class first and sucked up to teachers and tried to make friends by following other kids around, trying way too hard to be funny and cute and popular. She's always made a point to say that kindness is underrated, and goes out of her way to help other people, whether they asked for it or not—to the point where a lot of the kids in our class still think she's sort of annoying. But after the first year, Florence got pissed at the way others were treating Ash, and invited her to sit with us in the greenhouse at lunch. We've been hanging out ever since.

I've gotten to know Ashley—and even if she's trying too hard, at least she's trying. It's always hard to say no to her.

She grips my elbow and begins to shake it. I'm pretty sure I'm going to end up with a second broken arm. "Come on," she says. "Please?"

"Okay. All right!"

She grins. "Thank you, Nate!"

She follows Gideon out of the greenhouse.

Florence comes up behind me, staring after Ashley. "What was that all about?"

I shake my head. "You don't want to know."

4

THE MOVIE TODAY IS *AMÉLIE*—MY NINTH FAVORITE FILM of all time. Maybe I'll ask Flo to draw Audrey Tautou on my cast next. Classic: incredible characters, a story spun from the iconic scene of Amélie learning about the death of Princess Diana and dropping her perfume stopper, causing her to bend down and find the loose tile that hides a mysterious box of a child's tokens, which leads her on an adventure to find its owner and help as many people as she can, allowing her to feel love and acceptance for the first time.

The moderator who's supposed to be in the room with us at all times basically doesn't give a fuck and leaves us in the room alone, lights off, projector manipulated so that it's propped up and aimed at the ceiling. The desks have all been cleared, and blankets and pillows pulled from the closet just for this occasion have been plopped on the cold tile floor. We pile on top of the blankets and pillows and each other, and *Amélie* plays on the ceiling with its English subtitles while a bag of greasy popcorn makes its way around and Theo and Winona make out in their own personal corner, as they always do.

Florence lies down on one side of me. She puts her head on my chest, the way she would before she cheated on me with Lydia over the summer, when we came to film club instead of going to her place to make out, and she doesn't seem to think anything's wrong with this, so I decide nothing's wrong with it either. I just hope she doesn't notice how hard or fast my heart is beating, because it'd be a little embarrassing if she did.

My broken arm is at my side out of harm's way, but Oliver James keeps glancing at me like he's nervous he's going to roll over onto it. I put a hand on his arm to let him know it's all right. He looks at me in surprise, his cheeks red. He takes a big breath and shifts into his pillow. As humiliating as it was for Gideon to announce earlier, it's true—Ollie's pretty effing cute. He stares up at the ceiling, so I do too. I'm really comfortable with Florence resting against me. Even when we were just lying in bed together, not kissing or dry humping or anything, it felt like we always fit together perfectly. After that whole thing with Lydia, she'd ask me why I wasn't more mad. But I was angry—I just forced myself to forgive her. Told myself that I loved her too much to let it come between us. I put my good arm over her shoulder and I can feel her smiling against my chest.

Ollie's stopped moving around. He stares up at the ceiling, this glossy look in his eyes, and when the scene of fifteen orgasming Parisians flashes, he laughs with everyone else. I wonder if he's never seen *Amélie* before. If he'd stayed here, I would've made him watch it with me at least twenty times. If he'd stayed . . . Well, a lot of things might've been different, but that doesn't matter now.

He must feel me staring at him, because he looks at me. He doesn't give me a weird look or anything, like it's perfectly normal I'd be staring at him in the dark when we're supposed to be watching a movie. I snap my gaze back up to the ceiling, but heat's coming from his arm, close enough that I can practically feel it through my cast.

Florence shifts on my chest, and I realize that my arm around her has fallen asleep. "You okay?" she whispers.

I nod. "Yeah, of course."

We go back to watching the movie.

The bright sky has streaks of green in it by the time *Amélie* is finished, and everyone's feeling good and happy and a little in love with each other, since movies have this way of connecting us all and making us share the same emotion, like we might as well be the same person. I don't know—maybe I'm just feeling weird because I got to cuddle with Florence for two hours.

We amble outside, trees and ground damp, scent of fresh rain still hanging in the air. Theo and Winona head off, and Emma and Lucas and a few others linger behind, talking and laughing about their favorite scenes, but it's already almost six p.m., and I have to leave if I want to make my mom's seven o'clock curfew. I try to ignore the growing frustration at being the only person here who has to hurry home.

Florence hooks her arm with mine. "Wanna come over?" she asks. "Watch Netflix? Maybe I can draw Amélie on your cast."

She grins at me, because she knows she read my mind, but I hesitate. He isn't looking at me or anything, but I can see Ollie hanging back, hands in his pockets as he scuffs his sneaker against the wet pavement, waiting for me so that we can walk home together—and while I'd kind of take *any* excuse to avoid walking back with Oliver James, I know I have to face him eventually. "Sorry, Flo. I should get home."

She looks surprised. "Oh. Okay." She hesitates. "Everything's okay with us, right?"

She'll ask that sometimes. I know she's worried that we've been walking over a thin sheet of ice hand in hand for the past few months. The weight of everything between us—that she cheated on me with Lydia, that we broke up and pretend everything's normal, that I'm still in love with her and she might still be in love with me—is going to be too heavy for us.

The ice is cracking beneath our feet. I know that's what she's worried about, because I'm pretty worried about it, too.

"Yeah," I say. "Everything's fine. It's just my mom's curfew—it's stupid, but I'm going to be late if I go to your place."

"Okay." She rubs her arms and shrugs. "Good night, Bird."

"See you tomorrow," I tell her, watching as she makes her way in the opposite direction. I don't know why I feel like I'm betraying her.

Oliver's watching me now. I take a deep, shaky breath and walk over.

He cracks his knuckles. "Is it okay if I go back with you?"

I wonder if he's secretly hoping I'll say no, that I'll walk home ten feet in front of him without speaking, and that tomorrow we can just pretend this never happened—never talk to each other again. A part of me would prefer that to this bumblefuck of awkwardness.

But still, I nod. "Yeah, of course it's okay."

We start walking.

"I've wanted to talk to you all day," Oliver says. He points at me, holds his right fist to his mouth with the thumb under his nose, brings it down to clap the left hand over, points at me again. One of the first signs he taught me when we were kids.

"Hide from you?" I force a laugh. "Why would I do that?"

Ollie doesn't answer, and I can't tell if it's because he didn't read my lips or if it's because he doesn't want to respond. He tells me, "I'm really happy to be back. I missed Seattle."

I want to ask if he missed me also, but I'm not that brave. "I mean. Santa Fe must've been cool too." I pause. "It must suck to be away from your boyfriend."

Oliver frowns. "What'd you say?"

I pull my phone out of my pocket. It's a weird thing to type out, and typing with one hand is painfully slow, but I hold out the phone when I'm done.

Oliver takes the phone, reads, and hands it back. "We're texting every day and video chatting after school." That's all he says about it.

He's quiet. Waiting for me to get to the real reason we're walking together. Especially since all this awkwardness is because of me. I take a deep breath, thumb moving a little more quickly over my screen, hand him my phone. I'm sorry for the way things ended.

He reads, but doesn't say anything.

I swallow. I was pretty young. It was just stupid kid stuff.

He stops, and I turn to face him. "Stupid kid stuff?"

"I mean, the day you left . . . I—ah—did something. I shouldn't have. I know that now, but I was just a kid, and I had no idea what would happen, and I guess it was just the stress of thinking I'd never see or speak to you again. I thought I felt some things for you, so I freaked out and did something

45

weird. And I fucked up our friendship."

I bite my lip to shut myself up, and he watches my mouth, shaking his head. "That was a lot. I have no idea what you said." His tone is tight with frustration.

It's a frustration I feel too. I wish I remembered the sign language he taught me. I point at him and me. "Us. Our friendship. I messed it up."

He hesitates, looks away. "Maybe you did. I don't know."

That hurts. I wasn't really expecting him to agree with me.

He glances up at me through his lashes. His lashes have always been pretty long. "Did you say you felt some things?"

Of all the things for him to read correctly—I hesitate, mouth open, heart about to leap out of my chest. It's actually easier to type this one on my phone. **It was just a stupid little crush.** He looks at me as he hands the phone back. I put the peace sign up to my forehead for good measure. "A dumb kid crush. I'm sorry I made things weird."

He takes in another breath, looking off down the street with that serious stare of his, squinting into the distance like any film protagonist would. He used to intimidate me. When we first met in elementary school as kids, he never smiled or laughed. I just thought he didn't like me. But I eventually realized that most times, people don't smile because they're happy, or laugh because they think something's funny. They do it because they want someone else to like them, or because they don't know what to say, or because they're nervous, or because they're being polite. Oliver James—he's just too honest with himself to hide behind a smile that isn't real. And when he watches me with that stare of his, it's obvious he expects the same.

The green in the sky is becoming a darker blue. He glances at me. "Let's keep going."

I walk beside him, trying not to think back to the day we said goodbye, the day he left for New Mexico. We'd been at his house, in his bedroom. He sat on his bed cross-legged, hugging a pillow, while I lay sprawled out on his floor, neither of us speaking or signing. What do you say to your best friend when you know there's a chance you're never going to see him again? He was looking anywhere but me. His mom came inside, gave us a sad smile, and signed to Ollie that it was time to go. She said she'd be outside and walked back down the hall.

"I'll text you," Ollie said, still not looking at me, like he didn't want to know what I'd have to say.

I didn't want to cry, so I jumped up and grabbed him and tried to force the pillow over his face, and he started laughing and shouting and kicking out. We both fell hard to the floor, still laughing—Ollie's eyes all wet and red, maybe not just because falling had hurt. We just lay there for a second, grinning, and I leaned forward and kissed him. It was my first. His too, I'm pretty sure. It lasted as long as the blink of Oliver's eyes as he pulled back, mouth open. He didn't say anything. Just stared, his face and ears becoming a blotchy red. He leapt to his feet and ran out the door without another word. I tried to follow, to grab his hand and apologize and try to explain, tell him I was just joking. He ran outside to his mom. I still remember the expression on Mrs. Hernández's face—her confusion as Oliver James signed to her that I was leaving. We didn't say goodbye.

I texted Oliver when I got home, but he didn't answer me. I messaged him a few times, but he didn't respond at all. I figured it was because he hated me. And so, in just three seconds, I managed to eff up our entire seven-year-long friendship.

"I'm sorry," he says, rubbing his fist in a circle on his chest. "I should've answered your emails. Your text messages. Something."

I face him, unbroken hand in my hoodie's pocket, walking backward. "It's okay. All in the past, right?" I say, even though a part of me wants to ask why he didn't answer.

He points at himself, points his finger at his chin, points at me. "I've missed you, Bird."

I try to ignore the beating in my chest that's gotten considerably louder. "I've missed you too."

Ollie smirks. "Apparently not that much, if you didn't recognize me."

"What?"

"At the coffee shop," he says, smiling with those full-blown dimples. Maybe the first time he's really smiled at me all day. "I helped you clean up your hot chocolate, but you didn't recognize me."

I feign an offended expression and hand him my phone. **In my defense, you look COMPLETELY different.**

He puts his index finger to his lips before extending it to me, hooks the same finger into a question mark. "Really?"

Well—not really, I guess. His dimples are the same. His brown curls. That shine in his eyes.

"To be honest, I didn't actually recognize you at first either," he admits. "I thought you looked familiar, but it wasn't until school that I put two and two together, since I figured you might be there."

I'm getting a little faster at typing on my phone now. **See? You had the upper hand.** I smile at him while he laughs. **Plus, I don't look that different.**

"You're kidding, right? You grew, like, five feet." I roll my eyes, and when he laughs, I feel a warmth spread through me.

We keep walking until we reach the bend in our neighborhood. We'll get to my house first in a minute or two, but I don't want to go home yet. I'm happy I'm having an actual human interaction with Oliver James. We're quiet as we cross the street. I have so many questions, so many things I want to talk to him about, but I don't know where to start.

Ollie opens his mouth to speak but then closes it, glancing at me.

49

I turn my palms upward and shake them back and forth. "What is it?"

He swallows, staring at the ground. "I'm sorry if it's not okay to ask this. . . ." He looks up again. "Today's the anniversary, right?"

I didn't really expect Ollie to remember something like that. "Yeah, today's the anniversary."

He actually looks concerned, as if five years haven't passed at all. Like we're still the best friends we once were. "Are you okay?"

"Uh. Yeah." I grab my phone and type, handing it to him. **It's weird. It's like sometimes I forget he's gone. Other times the pain is still fresh.**

He nods, handing me back my phone. "I know what you mean." Ollie's grandfather died when we were kids. He helped me a lot when my dad died because he knew what I was going through.

I can see my house up ahead, and I catch myself slowing my pace. Ollie smooths a flat palm down the length of his arm, points two index fingers together, places his knuckles together with the thumbs pointing up and turns them toward me. "How'd you hurt your arm?"

Now I'm embarrassed. I hold the cast to my side with my other hand. "I fell off a roof."

"Wait, what?"

I type it, hand him the phone. Ollie presses his lips together like he's struggling to hold in a laugh. Struggling—and losing. "Jesus, how'd that happen?"

I was over at Florence's, and her cat got up onto the roof and was too afraid to come down, so I tried to go up after her. It didn't end well. Flo wouldn't stop apologizing for like an entire week.

Ollie smiles as he reads. "That's nice of you." He touches the cast. I feel myself jolt, almost as if he's touching my skin, but hold the arm up so he doesn't think I'm pulling away. He traces the fresh Tina, holds his hand to his face as though putting on a mask and swipes his hand back and forth. "These are amazing."

"Favorite characters from movies," I start to say, but realize he isn't looking at me. I'm nervous to try, because I haven't done it in a long time and I've never really been good at ASL, but it's shitty to make Oliver lip-read and look at phones all day. I fingerspell F-L-O and put my left palm up, let my index finger move over the palm as if drawing. Ollie holds up his own left hand, but uses his pinky to draw instead, correcting me.

"Thanks," I say.

He nods. "She's really good."

We've stopped in front of my house. Ollie looks at it with this nostalgic expression. I wonder if it looks the same to him.

I hand him my phone. **I'm glad you ended up at Bastard.**

Ollie raises an eyebrow, hands back the phone. Shit. Fucking autocorrect.

Sorry, BALLARD. I wouldn't have known you were back.

Ollie nods. "My mom wanted to send me up to Northwest. Same story, you know."

I did know. When we were kids, at the end of every single summer, Ollie's mom would try to convince Oliver James to start attending Northwest School for the Deaf. Said he'd learn better, being in his own community, his own culture. To be honest, I wondered if she was right—and it wasn't like the school was out of state. It's only a fifteen-minute drive away. We'd still see each other after school and on weekends. Not a big deal at all. But every time his mom suggested Ollie change schools, it became this huge thing with angry signing and Ollie refusing to speak, until finally his mom gave up again.

I never really got why Ollie refused to go. I'm afraid of saying something stupid and ignorant, the way most hearing people do, but I try signing, pointing both index fingers up and then toward him, bringing my hand to my forehead and putting it into the Y symbol. "Why'd you always refuse to go?"

He shrugs. "I guess, when I was a kid, I didn't like the idea of being completely defined by my identity. Besides, I thought I already had the community I needed." He glances at me and looks at my mouth, like he's waiting for me to speak. When I don't, he says, "I almost let her convince me to go this time."

"Seriously?"

"You look surprised."

"That's because I'm very surprised."

He laughs. "You're still really funny."

I hand him my phone. **Not really. It's just my deadpan delivery. It works in my favor.**

He glances up at me through his lashes as he hands the phone back. Now he's looking at me in the same nostalgic way. The look barely lasts a second. He turns his head away. "It makes sense, I guess. Going to Northwest. But I decided it's easier to stick to what I know."

"Yeah. Makes sense."

Ollie doesn't see me respond. He pauses. "Have you been practicing ASL all this time?"

I hesitate. After Oliver James got sick and started teaching me signs, I kept learning on my own, too, watching videos online. I liked it—ASL's pretty cool—and it felt important to know the same language my best friend used. But I stopped practicing after I fucked up everything between us.

I shake my head. "No. Practicing wouldn't have been as fun without you."

He gives me this surprised look, stares at me like he's trying to figure out what I mean by that, and I look at him too, taking him in. He's definitely pretty cute—I can understand why Ashley wants to put him in her pocket. Speaking of Ash . . . I groan and roll my eyes.

He laughs. "What's wrong?"

I point at the ground, cup my hand into a C and turn it

downward in front of my face, outline a question mark with my finger. "This is a weird question."

"Go for it."

I sigh, pulling out my phone. **How do you feel about Ashley?**

His face is blank for a second. "Ashley Perkins? She's nice. Why?"

I feel like an idiot, but I know Ash will ask me about this tomorrow, and I can already feel the sting of her hands on my unbroken arm (and maybe my broken one, too) if I don't have an answer for her. I type on my phone's screen. **Would you want to go out with her?**

Ollie makes a face like he's trying not to laugh, and I have to admit, I feel like I've gone backward a few years into junior high. "Did she ask you to ask me that?"

I nod, stewing in my shame.

He can't hold the laughter in anymore. He points at me, rubs his right palm over his left. "That's sweet of you."

I was pretty sure she was going to break my other arm if I didn't.

"Well," he says, and his smile starts to fade. "I like her, but I guess she's not really my type. Besides, Aiden and I said we'd only see each other." He shrugs. "I still want to be her friend, though."

"Yeah, understandable," I tell him—though I guess it'll suck to be the messenger of bad news tomorrow.

Ollie cracks his knuckles, glancing at a car that speeds by. He said Ash wasn't his type—and I can't help but feel a little curious. What *is* his type, then? What does he like about Aiden that he didn't like about me? It's probably better not to ask. And the little pinch of jealousy—that's just asshole behavior, so I try to ignore that too.

We stand there in front of my house—not moving, not speaking or signing. Ollie takes in a big breath. "I was really happy to see you today, Bird."

"Yeah. It was great seeing you too."

"It's been a really long time. Five years."

"Yeah."

He won't look away. He's never been ashamed to watch me, patiently waiting for a response—but I can't think of anything else to say. "I guess I'll see you tomorrow."

"Okay. See you tomorrow."

We both stand there a little longer before he signs a goodbye and starts walking up the hill. I stay there a second too long, just watching his back, until I open the door, step into the foyer, and shut the door behind me.

Holy shit.

I don't know what I was expecting to happen today, but this—seeing Oliver James for the first time in five years—definitely was not it.

I start to head upstairs, but I see my mom sprawled across the couch, flipping through TV channels. I take a breath, walk over into the living room that smells like pizza. A half-eaten pie in its box lies on the floor. I plop down next to her on the couch, fabric tearing a little at the seams. She gives me a surprised look, but doesn't say anything as she aims the remote at the TV.

"You okay?" I ask her.

She nods, and her eyes are red, and I'm pretty sure she was just crying.

"Did you end up visiting the cemetery?"

"Around noon. It was emptier than usual."

I don't know what to say. I never know what to say. But maybe that's okay. Maybe just being here is enough.

"Is it okay if I watch TV with you?"

She smiles a little, still clicking the remote. "If you insist."

5

MY BEDROOM'S CEILING SLANTS DOWN SO THAT WHEN I was a kid I'd hit my head whenever I jumped on my bed. There are shelves covering the red walls, filled with books stacked horizontally and collectible VHS tapes and empty DVD cases and vinyl records—and all over the walls are posters from my favorite movies and yellowed tickets taped up and drawings. I toe off my ratty Converses into the pile of shoes by my door and climb into bed to start up my laptop just as I get a text from my sister: **Google Hangouts?**

When I log on, Rebecca's sitting expectantly in front of her screen, her dorm with its bunk bed and Christmas lights in the background even though it's only September. Becca left early for summer classes, and after only one month, I miss her more than I thought I would. We look really similar: same wide mouth and dark brown eyes, same dark brown skin and thick black hair. She's got hers out, curls fanning around her face like a halo. Becca said I needed a new style, so as a parting gift, she shaved my sides and left a tangle of thick curls on top. She says it looks good. I'm going to have to trust her on that.

"Where've you been?" She waggles her eyebrows. "Flo's?"

"Shut up."

"First day of junior year was today, right?" She wipes away a fake tear. "My little brother is growing up."

"Talk to you later, Becks—"

"No, wait," she says, waving her hands around. "Let me give you some advice. It's what big sisters are supposed to do."

I roll my eyes. "Fine."

"First: be nice."

"What? I'm nice. Why would you say that? I'm always nice."

She smile-winces at me. "You can be a little standoffish sometimes. I don't think you realize you're doing it. Just—you know. Be nice."

I don't even know what to say to that. I'm not standoffish. Quiet, maybe, because I like to gather my thoughts before I just spit them out—and sure, fine, I can be a little shy sometimes. Who isn't? And—all right, I'm awkward as hell. . . . But I'm never *standoffish*. That makes me sound like a hermit who lives alone in the woods and shoots a rifle at anyone who comes within twenty feet of his property. But if I tried to convince her otherwise, I know Becca would just smile and nod at me like I'm a kid throwing a tantrum.

"Second: don't decide you're not good enough to apply to colleges for screenwriting. You *are* good enough, and you *do* deserve to get in."

I rub the back of my neck. She's heard plenty of my whining about the college hunt. "There's no way you can tell if I deserve it or not."

"You're passionate and hardworking. You've loved movies since forever. And I mean *really* loved them. You wouldn't stop talking about *Eternal Sunshine of the Spotless Mind* for months."

"Eighth favorite movie of all time."

"See?" she says, breaking into an infectious grin. "Some people are just made for things. You're made for this." She leans back, still smiling. "Dad would take us to see a movie every Sunday. You remember that?"

I try not to think of it, because I always get a little emotional when I do, but the flashbacks roll in anyway—my dad's big hand holding mine, crossing the street to the Ridgemont, buying a bag of popcorn for us to share. "Yeah, I remember."

Her smile fades. "Today's the anniversary."

"I know."

"Have you spent time with Mom?"

"I don't really know what to say."

"Me neither. Sometimes it still feels like it only just happened."

We're both quiet for a while. I tell Becca, "You know, something weird happened today."

"What's that?"

"Do you remember Oliver James? The guy who lived on top of the hill?"

She laughs. "Do I remember Oliver James? Of course I do. You two were obsessed with each other."

"We weren't *obsessed*."

"You were pretty obsessed."

"We weren't obsessed!"

"Yeah, okay," she says, giving her best Jennifer Lawrence impression. "What about him?"

I hesitate, even though there's really only one way to say it. "He moved back."

She leans into the laptop. "Really? Have you spoken to him yet?"

"Yeah. He's back at Ballard and everything. I just—don't really know what to say to him either."

She takes a deep breath. "Well, my final piece of advice: don't overthink things. Just relax. Do and say exactly what you feel. Enjoy life while you still don't have to worry about college exams."

I roll my eyes, but I guess that's pretty good advice.

After Becca tells me goodnight, I open my Slugline writing

program and stare at the screen. I've been trying to write my first script for the past year, and so far, all I have are twelve half-finished stories—each and every single one of them complete crap. I know I'm not very good at this, but whenever someone asks me what my life plans are, screenwriting is all I can picture myself doing. Robert McKee's *Story* is on my nightstand like it's a bible, and Blake Snyder's *Save the Cat!* is on my bookshelf, beside *Bird by Bird* by Anne Lamott. I've read them all about twenty times now. Problem is, books can't give me talent. And I'm really not sure I have any.

I close the program, click on a webpage, and go to Netflix.

It's only the second day, and I'm already over school. It's just more of the same bullshit—teachers giving more homework than necessary, trying to scare us into freaking out about our futures, shoving information we'll never need or use down our throats. Except this time, Oliver James is there, permanently in the corner of my eye in the courtyard and in the halls and during lunch with his red cheeks and dimples and steadfast gaze.

Apparently I'm not the only one he's having an effect on. I walk past Ashley and Gideon, heads together and talking (probably about *Halo* strategy)—but when Ash sees me, she jumps up and follows me inside, grabbing my unbroken arm and pulling me into a nook that's usually reserved for quick make-out sessions before class.

"So," she says, "have you spoken to Oliver James for me yet?"

I'm having a hard time meeting her eye. "Oh, yeah—I spoke to him last night."

She waits expectantly. "Well?"

"Uh—sorry, Ash. He said he's not interested."

Her face blanks. "What? Are you sure? I mean, really sure?"

I can't blame her for being surprised. Ashley has the sort of study-hard-get-straight-As kind of attitude that usually means she gets what she wants, if she really puts her mind to it—but I don't think she's realized that people aren't as straightforward.

"Yeah, I'm sure. He and his boyfriend are only seeing each other."

She lifts her chin. "Well, I have no choice but to accept that, right?" She sighs and shrugs. "Thanks for asking, Bird."

The end of the day finally comes, and Flo and I are walking toward the row of bikes chained up to the metal fence so that I can ride over to her place—but Ollie's waiting on a bench across the courtyard. He waves, tugs his ear. He cups two upward palms, pulling them toward his chest, points two index fingers at his chest, pats a hand to his chest, steeples his hands and squares them into the shape of a house, hooks his finger into a question mark.

I hesitate and turn to Flo. "Hey—is it okay if I take a rain check? If I come over, I'll end up staying pretty late, and I don't want to piss off my mom."

She looks from me to Ollie and back to me. "We'll just pay attention to the time. We have a solid four hours of Netflix before you have to leave."

"Yeah. I guess I'm just a little tired. Another time?"

"I mean—yeah, sure."

I grin, but even I know it's not really reaching my eyes. I'm a crappy liar, and maybe an even crappier friend. "I'll talk to you later, all right?"

She nods, still looking between me and Oliver James, before she walks off in her own direction. Ollie follows me to the bikes, and I unlock mine to walk it beside him.

6

OLLIE AND I TRUDGE UP THE HILL TO HIS HOUSE, MY LEGS
burning—but before long I find myself walking the same path
like I hadn't stopped walking it five years ago. A couple of
things have changed, but mostly everything is the same: the
white fence with the overgrown rosebush, the tree growing in
the middle of the sidewalk, breaking up the cement so I have
to be careful not to trip over the roots, and then finally Ollie's
house, the smallest one on the street.

He opens the door, and a huge gray Labradoodle comes
scrambling. Ollie tries to wrestle her into a sitting position, but
she just ends up leaning against him. We manage to get around
her and into the house, and he closes the door behind us.

Surprisingly, the inside hasn't changed at all from when
we were kids, except in the way that houses look smaller as

you get older. It even still smells the same: like freshly burnt incense, though I've never seen any, and lavender. The living room has the same furniture—same stained floral sofa, same wooden coffee table. They must've taken it to Santa Fe and brought it all the way back. Ollie's mother never sold the house, and I was happy about that. I'd never get used to the idea of strangers living in Ollie's home.

The kitchen is right next to the living room. A shadow moves—and there's Mrs. Hernández with her curling brown hair and brown eyes and wide smile. I'm pretty sure Ollie has less than .99 percent of his dad's DNA. She comes in, wiping her hands on a towel that she tosses onto the counter.

"Nathan," she says, wrapping her arms around me and kissing both cheeks. She switches to signing, but she signs so fast that I can't read everything she's saying. I'm glad when she translates out loud also. "Look at you. You're so handsome now."

I glance at Ollie, expecting him to look kind of embarrassed, but he just grins at his mom. I forgot—he's the only guy I know who's almost never embarrassed by his parents. He moves into the kitchen to grab a dog bowl, turns on the faucet, puts it down again with a clatter.

Mrs. Hernández crosses her arms. "I told Ollie to bring you by tonight. I just had to get a look at you. Look at how tall you've gotten!"

My smile wavers. It kind of feels like Ollie only asked me to come over because his mom told him to. Ollie scratches the

Labradoodle behind her ears.

"Don't mind me," Mrs. Hernández says, fingers still flying through the air. "I know you two have some catching up to do. I'm just leaving. Ollie, text me if you need anything, all right?" She grabs him by the collar and pulls him in to give him a swift kiss on the cheek, and then she's out the door. A second later, I hear the car out front start up and rumble down the street.

"She teaches night classes now," Ollie explains. We stand there a second longer, Ollie still scratching his dog's ears. "This is Donna Noble," he says, looking up at me.

"Donna Noble? From *Doctor Who*?"

He nods. "Best show ever created, hands down. Well—until Matt Smith's last season, anyway. Things really went downhill for a while."

"Oh, come on—no one ever gives Peter Capaldi a chance."

"You *would* like the grumpy old man," he says, laughing.

"What's that supposed to mean?"

He keeps laughing, and I can't help but grin. I wipe my hands off on the back of my jeans before putting them in my hoodie's pockets so that it'll look like I'm not freaking out, even though that's exactly what I'm doing. Just the thought of no parents in the house, being left alone . . . there's something about the idea that makes me a little too excited, and I hope to God Ollie doesn't notice, because there'd be nothing more humiliating than Ollie seeing my halfway hard-on.

"Let's head to my bedroom," Ollie says—but then he hesitates, glancing at me, like we were both hit by the same memory of the last time I was there.

I don't trust myself to actually say anything, so I just nod and follow Ollie down the hall—same hall, same bedroom with its plain blue walls. He hasn't unpacked a whole lot yet. His bed is made, and his desk has his laptop and a book by Benjamin Sáenz. Boxes are stacked up against the walls, which are still bare except for some black-and-white photos: plains and fields and a mountain in the distance. A shot of an old town, abandoned car on the side of the street. A woman with a wrinkled face, her neck and shoulders covered in tattoos.

There're color photos, too: a group of kids around our age, sitting in green grass, laughing. Another of them looking over their shoulders on a bus. The obligatory jumping shot with the sun shining yellow behind them. There's one guy who's in them over and over again, and just one close-up photo of him also: he's white and has straw-colored hair, brown eyes, freckles. Aiden, I'm assuming. There's a twist in my gut.

"Did you take these yourself?" I ask, glad for the distraction and desperate for something to talk about, but Ollie isn't looking at me, so I wave my hand until he glances over, surprised. I ask the question again.

He stands beside me. "Yeah."

"They're really good."

He blushes. "Thanks. There's something amazing about

67

capturing an entire story in just one second," he says. He makes the sign for "amazing," hand waving over his face, taps his two index fingers together, and signs a word I don't understand. He says aloud, "Amazing, and really hard to do. I don't know. I'm not as good as I want to be."

I kind of get it. Even though screenwriters have more than a few seconds to capture an entire story, it still feels impossible sometimes.

Ollie points at the color photo of the park. "These are some of my friends. This one's Aiden."

The twist in my gut is almost painful now. I point at my nose, point my finger straight out, and hook it into a question mark.

Ollie squints at me. "What?"

I swallow hard. Was it a weird question to ask? "Do you miss him?"

Realization crosses his face. "Oh—this is *miss*." He points at his chin.

"Oh. Right. Sorry."

He shakes his head. "Nothing to be sorry about. And yeah, I do. This is the first time either of us are trying long-distance, and he's been texting me pretty much nonstop, but I'm afraid of messing this up."

"How would you mess it up?"

He shrugs, mumbles something I don't understand. He adds, "Aiden's great, though. He was really shy and never spoke to me very much, and then a year ago he asked me out, kind of out of nowhere. He said he'd had a crush on me for a while."

Donna Noble makes herself comfortable by the edge of the bed and looks at me expectantly, thumping her tail when I scratch her behind the ears. Ollie sits down too. He doesn't ask me to sit, and I don't think that's a good idea anyway. It's weird that I got this excited just because I got asked to his bedroom, and because—I mean, yeah, he's pretty cute—and I need to get a handle on myself.

"Where's your dad?" He doesn't see me trying to speak. I wave my hand until he looks up at me, then sign the question, my flat palm up and thumb tapping my forehead, shaking my index finger back and forth, my hand feeling too big and awkward.

Ollie clenches his jaw. "He's in New Mexico. My parents got a divorce last month."

My mouth falls open. "Shit."

"It's been a while coming."

I tap my head, extending my hand up, shaking my head. "I didn't know."

I mean, I guess I did know it was a while coming. Ollie would sleep over at my place at least once a week, and 90 percent of the time it was to escape his mom and dad's fighting. That's basically the image I have of Mr. and Mrs. Hernández: yelling at each other. All of the time. The idiot in me used to get mad at them . . . and at Oliver James. Ollie's dad was still alive. I thought they should've been more grateful for that.

"Jesus." I move a fist in a circle around my chest. "I'm sorry."

"That's why we moved back. I have to go back to Santa Fe on holidays, though. My dad's trying to convince me to live with him permanently."

My heart drops. "Do you think you will?"

He shrugs. "I don't know. It's all so hard and complicated. But I'm actually kind of relieved they got a divorce." He says something I don't understand, but he doesn't notice—keeps speaking. "They wouldn't stop fighting. I couldn't escape it. And they'd try to get me into the middle of it too. My mom would try to get me to do things to hurt my dad, and he'd say she wasn't a good mother."

I cross my arms. God, I'm a piece of shit. I didn't know any of this was happening. Didn't even know this was the reason he'd moved back. I know he doesn't mean for me to feel guilty, but that's exactly how I feel. Ollie was always there for me when we were kids. After my dad died, whenever I felt like I was going a little crazy because I started to get scared I was going to die too, whenever I just didn't want to be alone . . . Ollie was always there. I should've been there for him.

"I'm sorry," I say again. Sign it. Wish there was a way to telepathically communicate it, so he could actually feel how sorry I am.

"Don't apologize. You didn't do anything."

I sit down on the bed next to him. "I fucked everything up."

"What'd you say?"

I'm too lazy to reach for my bag and look for my phone, so I point to his Android, resting on his nightstand. He leans over, puts in the passcode, hands it to me without looking. There's a text from Aiden: **Hey, what're you doing?**

I hesitate. Ollie turns his palms upward, shakes them back and forth.

I swipe away from the message and open his notes app, trying not to feel like a homewrecker. I type quickly and hand Ollie the phone. **I ruined our friendship.**

Oliver James is watching me carefully. "I could've texted you back."

I can't really blame you. I point at myself, cup my hand into a *C* by my face and turn it downward. "I made things weird."

No parents in the house, alone in his bedroom, sitting beside each other, Ollie watching me. "It wasn't weird."

My heart's pounding harder. "Really?"

"If anything, the way I reacted was weird." He shrugs. "I just freaked out because I was a kid, and I didn't know what to do, and I didn't know how I felt." He keeps watching me. "I was so dramatic."

We don't talk or sign or anything for a while. I'm just sitting there, and Oliver's looking at me, waiting for me to speak, like he isn't embarrassed to be staring at all. I fiddle with the phone before I muster the courage to type and show him the screen. **Can I ask you something?**

He nods.

It's okay if you don't want to tell me, but I've always wondered, since you never actually said anything. Always wondered how you did feel about it, or if you might've felt the same way. He looks up at me, frowning as he cradles the phone. I pause. "Did you?"

He's squinting, like he isn't sure what I said. "Did I what?"

I bite my lip. "Feel the same way?"

Ollie looks away. "I don't know. You were my best friend, and suddenly you were . . ." He pinches his fingers together, puts them to his mouth and puts them to his other hand, ears turning red as he glances up at me.

I swallow, shame creeping up my neck. "Yeah. No, I get it. I shouldn't have even asked. All in the past, right?" That's what I say, even though I know it isn't all in the past, since I'm pretty sure my eleven-year-old crush has turned into a sixteen-year-old one.

Ollie tugs on his ear before he turns on the laptop resting on his nightstand and pulls it onto the bed. "You ever see that BuzzFeed article about toddlers basically being drunk adults?"

I don't want him to change the subject. I want to tell him that I'm feeling the same way again, that maybe I never stopped feeling this way—but then what? What could he possibly say to that? Besides, he has a boyfriend now. Maybe it really is easier to leave everything in the past.

Ollie's already gotten to the page. He's looking at me expectantly. "No, I haven't seen it," I tell him, "but it sounds pretty hilarious."

After cracking up at that, we look at a ton of Tumblr posts. We spread out on his bed, arms bumping into each other, and Tumblr posts become music videos, which turns into just music. Ollie told me once that for him, music is a new experience now—feeling the vibrations through his skin, against his ears. Anything with drums and bass is his favorite. We end up scrolling through Pandora stations, going from Ellie Goulding to Lorde to Santigold, talking and signing and typing on our phones about nothing—*Doctor Who*, my favorite movies, the script I've been trying to write.

"Script?"

"Yeah. I want to be a screenwriter."

Ollie sits up. "I didn't know that. It makes sense, though. You've always loved movies." He watches me carefully. "I bet you're really good at it."

I rub the back of my neck, sit up also. "That's nice of you, but I need to actually finish writing a script first."

I'm not sure Ollie caught what I said. "Hey—you know, there's this thing, this contest called Emerging Creatives," he says, lying back down beside me again, opening a new tab and typing a web address so that the site pops up. I lean forward to see. "One of my teachers told me about it back in Santa Fe. A college is offering high school students university-level classes in the arts. They're accepting ten students, but if you apply and win first place, you get a full scholarship—everything included. Tuition. Room and board."

"Holy crap."

Ollie doesn't see me speaking. He starts to read the classes listed. "Painting. Photography." He looks at me. "I'm applying for that one." Goes back to reading. "And filmmaking." He clicks on the link, starts to scroll through the site. "They have screenwriting classes too." He turns back to me. "You should apply."

I mean, it sounds amazing—but . . . "I don't know." I pick up his phone again, turn the screen to him. **Won't I have to turn in a sample or something?**

Oliver goes back to reading the website, nods. "Yeah, you'd have to turn in a full-length script."

I give a sad little laugh. "Yeah—no. That's all right."

Ollie's smile fades. He puts his hand to his forehead, puts it into a Y shape before letting his thumb hit the underside of his chin and extending it.

I clutch my broken arm and its cast to my side. It's starting to ache again, my fingers tingling. "I mean—I'd never get in."

Ollie's full-on frowning now. "How do you know that?"

"I've never finished a script before." I twist the phone screen to him again. **I've tried to write like twelve different stories, but I always give up halfway through.**

Oliver James looks up at me. "So this is the perfect chance to finish your first script, then."

"Come on, Ollie." I pass him his phone again. **I'll be up** against kids who've probably had their scripts bought and sold and produced already.

"And that means they're better than you? No," he says when I try to interrupt. "You don't want to apply because you're scared you'll be told you're not good enough." I let out a sigh, roll my eyes more for the sake of him seeing me roll my eyes, but he keeps going. "What's the worst that'll happen?"

"Well. I mean. They could say no."

His fingertips bunched together extend from his chest. "And so what? It's not like that'll mean you can never write again. And," he says, "you'll have written your first script to apply. That'd be huge."

I can't exactly argue with that.

"On the other hand, if you do get in, you'd get an entire summer of free classes with professional screenwriters," he says. "If we're both accepted, we could go together." I know I can't say no to the possibility of spending an entire summer with Oliver James.

I let out a long sigh. "Okay. Fine. All right."

His gives me a wide smile. "The deadline's right after Thanksgiving. Think that's enough time?"

"It'll have to be, right?" Something occurs to me. "Where did you say this program was again?"

"What?"

I shake my index finger back and forth.

"Oh," he says, "it's in New York."

A laugh bubbles up. There's literally *no way in hell* my

mom would let me go to New York for the summer. Rebecca going to Chicago was bad enough, but New York is on the opposite end of the country. I don't think my mom would even let me go to Portland. I open my mouth to tell Oliver, but the time on the laptop catches my eye. Midnight.

"Holy crap," I say, scrambling from the bed. "My mom's going to freak out." I'm surprised she hasn't already called. I check my bag—either I left my phone at school, or it's on my nightstand in my bedroom.

Ollie's confused. He shakes his hands back and forth. "What's wrong?"

I grab his phone and toss it into his lap. **My mom gave me a seven o'clock curfew.**

"Oh, shit." He watches me fumble with my bag for a second. "Maybe you should just stay over—it's pretty late," Ollie says, and for a second, it really is like we just picked up where we left off. Except this time, he's also looking at me in a way that makes me wonder if we'd actually be doing a whole lot of sleeping.

I'm tempted to tell him yes. Maybe I could call my mom from his phone and tell her what happened, and by the time it's morning and I have to go back home, she'll have calmed down . . . but I know there's a bigger chance I'll just piss her off more. And besides that, something tells me that staying the night—here, in Ollie's bedroom—isn't the best idea in the world. I already effed up my friendship with Oliver James once. I'm not too eager to ruin it again.

I groan. "I can't. I'm already in enough trouble."

Ollie frowns, maybe not understanding what I said, and tugs on his ear before rubbing his fist in a circle around his chest. "I shouldn't have kept you here so late."

"No, it's not you. I wanted to be here." I realize that's kind of a weird thing to say, but it's too late to backtrack now. Ollie smiles. A little shyly, like he's blushing. Which makes me blush. And just leaves us blushing at each other.

He and Donna Noble walk me out of his bedroom and to the door.

"All right," I say, "so I'll see you tomorrow?"

He nods. "See you tomorrow, Bird."

Just as I figured, my mom's absolutely flipping her shit. For a split second I think I see my dad sitting in the living room, clicking through channels with the volume on mute while she paces around in the kitchen. I'm sixteen. I should be used to the idea that he's gone by now.

"Where the hell were you? Why didn't you call? Do you know how worried I was?" She stops her pacing, tying her bathrobe tightly, and faces me.

I'm a little too tired to deal with this right now. I lean against the kitchen archway and cross my arms. "Yeah, I think I have a pretty good idea."

She steps closer to me. "I thought you were dead. You know that, right?"

"That's a little dramatic."

She watches me, waiting for me to become an actual human being, but it isn't fair that she acts like this—lets her anxiety stop me from living my life.

"You can't be scared that I'm going to die every single time I step outside. You may be happy not living your life, but I want to live mine."

She straightens, hurt cascading over her face, and I know I'm officially the crappiest son on the planet. I rub my eyes. I don't even bother trying to explain that I was with Ollie. "I'm sorry. I didn't mean that."

She tells me I'm grounded for two weeks. "No more film club, no more hanging out with Florence—not if you can't make it home by seven. You go to school, and you come right back home. Is that clear?"

"Are you serious?"

She walks past me, into the living room, and leans against the back of the sofa, frowning. "What is this? A rebellious stage?"

"It's not rebellious to want some more freaking freedom!"

"Watch your mouth," she says, pointing at me.

I stare at the floor. "*Freaking* isn't even a bad word."

"Listen to me," she says. "I know things are difficult. Becca's off at college, and your dad—"

"I don't want to talk about Dad right now," I say shortly, looking away.

She takes a deep breath. "All right. Well, I miss him a lot.

I know it's been a few years, but grief never really goes away, and if you ever need to talk—I'm here." She puts up her hands defensively. "That's all I'm going to say about him tonight."

"Can I go to my room now?" I ask.

"Yes. Hey—wait." She taps her cheek, and I kiss it quickly and turn to go, but she holds on to my shoulder, and pulls me into a hug. The kind of hug I'd get as a kid. The kind of hug that let me know how loved I was, that I'd be safe as long as my mom's around. I start to get a little emotional, maybe because we were just talking about my dad, and when my mom pulls away her eyes are wet too. She rubs my back. "Love you, Nate."

"Love you too." I pause. "Am I still grounded?"

"Absolutely. See you in the morning."

I head upstairs. I guess I can see where my mom's coming from. She has a reason to be angry—and scared. She already lost her husband. It makes sense, I guess, that she'd be worried about losing her son too.

I look at my nightstand. Bull's-eye: there's my phone. It's not a big surprise that I didn't notice it wasn't in my bag all day. I'm not huge with phones and texting and social media. Florence calls me an old man when it comes to technology. I have Tumblr, but I only ever check it maybe once a week tops, and I don't have Twitter or Instagram or anything else. Being socially awkward in person is more than enough for me.

I turn my phone on and see I have sixteen missed calls.

Thirteen are from my mom. Three are from Florence. I have a few texts from her too. She says she really needs to talk to me. I text her back, asking what's wrong. The phone begins to ring a second later.

"Where the hell have you been?" she says.

Okay, I just heard this lecture. Definitely don't need to hear it again.

"I was out," I say, and I know my tone isn't coming out in the most polite way possible.

"Out?" she says again. "I thought you had to go home."

"I was just at Ollie's. I ended up walking him home, and he invited me inside."

Florence is silent on the other end.

"Flo? Are you there?"

Silence. The phone beeps, and when I pull it away, I see she ended the call. I drop it on my bed.

Fuckity fuck fuck.

7

FLORENCE ISN'T WAITING OUT AT OUR REGULAR SPOT ON
the bench the next morning. Gideon sits there with some of
his friends from soccer instead, shoulders hunched and his
face inches from a textbook he holds up to his face, reading
through our European history homework that's due in twenty
minutes. He catches my eye and gives me a grin that lets me
know I'm a dead man walking.

When I see Florence in the hall, her purple twists swinging
down her back, she ignores me.

"Flo—hey, Flo, wait!"

She just keeps marching forward, hugging a textbook to
her chest and with her backpack slung over her shoulder. It
takes me literally, actually standing right in front of her for her
to even look at me.

"Christ, Flo, what the hell is going on?"

She turns her full-blown *I am pissed* glare on me. And I can't really blame her. I was shitty to Florence. I blew her off and gave her crap for calling me out on it. I never really like it when it happens, but I can be an asshole sometimes.

"Look—I'm sorry," I tell her, and I automatically rub my fist in a circle on my chest too, which is stupid, since Flo doesn't know sign language. She stares at my hand over the rims of her glasses. I put my hand down. "I wasn't planning on staying at Ollie's so long, and I forgot my phone, so—"

She shakes her head and looks away, rolling her eyes. But I don't know if she's rolling her eyes at me, what I said, or at this whole situation. She won't look at me when she speaks. "Am I your best friend?" she asks.

The question catches me off guard. It's the needy, clingy sort of question Flo would usually be annoyed by—and I mean, don't get me wrong. I'm a needy, clingy sort of guy. Especially when it comes to Florence. But it's a little weird, because it's *not* her.

Flo watches me, waiting for a response. I swallow. "Yeah, of course you're my best friend. You know that."

She folds her arms. "I guess I'm just a little worried that—I don't know, you and Oliver James will go right back to being the best friends you were, and you'll forget all about me, especially after . . ." She pauses.

I don't need her to finish the sentence. "After everything with Lydia, you mean?"

She sighs. "I don't want to be your third wheel."

I automatically put my good arm over her shoulder and pull her in, and she wraps her arms around my waist. Warm, comfortable, fitting together perfectly like we always do. I feel like I could melt into her. "You're not a third wheel. You mean too much for that."

She nods against my chest. A few months ago, I would've bent down to kiss her, and we'd walk off into the sunset—but I know I have to let go now. She unravels her arms from me, giving the end of my hoodie a tug. She won't really look at me, and I realize there's something else—something she isn't telling me.

"What happened last night?" I ask her. "You said you needed to talk."

She shakes her head. "It's nothing. Forget about it."

I don't know if I believe that. I squint at her, but she won't meet my eyes. Flo isn't the kind of person to open up when she isn't ready to. If I try to force her, she'll just shut down.

I also don't know if I believe that we're back to being okay. This was a good scene on paper, I guess, but I've had the pleasure of knowing Flo for the past few years. We've been in fights before, and even after apologizing and agreeing to move on, she'll be a lot quicker to get into arguments for weeks afterward. *Forgive, not forget* would be her motto, I guess.

"Let's hang out today," she says.

I'm grounded. My mom will literally kill me if I don't come home right after school. But if I tell Florence no, I miss out on the chance to make things right. And, I don't know—the rules, the grounding. It all kind of pisses me off. Maybe my mom's right. Maybe I am going through some kind of rebellious phase.

"Okay. All right. What do you want to do?"

She smiles. "I'm in the mood for art."

Audrey Tautou smirks at me from my cast. I wish I didn't have to throw the thing away. Otherwise, I'd just hang it on my wall like it's a masterpiece.

Florence flops back on her bed, skirt riding up to show more of her legs, her thighs. I look up and see she's caught me staring, but she doesn't say anything about it.

"They're already killing us with homework," she says. "Let's just go back to summer, Bird."

"Summer before or after Lydia?"

"Before. Obviously."

"All right, I'll meet you about forty days ago."

She laughs. Keeps staring at her ceiling. I look at Audrey on my cast.

"You seem happy that Ollie's back," she says. She sounds genuinely curious about it, too, like we didn't just have an argument about him—but she doesn't look at me as she speaks. She busies herself with picking up a comic and flipping through its pages.

"Yeah, I guess I am. It's weird. It's not like I missed him all these years—only at first, right after he left." A twinge inside. Was that a lie? Am I lying to myself? Maybe I've missed Oliver James all along, and I just never realized it.

She finally drops the book and sits up to look at me. "Well, let me give you some free advice, Bird," she says.

"Free?"

"Yes, advice." She pats the bed beside her, and something tells me this isn't a good idea, but I never really listen to that something, do I? I sit down beside her, the bed sinking a little. "He's a really sweet guy. Don't fuck it up."

"That's your advice?"

"Yes, and it's good advice, too." Flo touches the elbow of my good arm. "I'm serious. It's always easy to let someone go out of insecurity or fear. I don't know—maybe he'll start to think you don't want to be his friend, and you'll start to think he's pulling away. Misunderstandings happen all the time, right?"

Yeah, but why would she think any of this would happen to me and Ollie?

"Just be careful with yourself," she says, and leans in to kiss my cheek. She does that all of the time, but today, her mouth lingers. Maybe that's just wishful thinking.

We're both quiet and looking into each other's eyes as if we're in some romantic drama.

"We never really had a misunderstanding," I tell her. "Things were good."

She smiles. "Yeah. I know."

The silence is pretty powerful. It makes me want to just get up and walk right out of her door. But I force myself to stay. Force myself to say, "I really didn't want it to end."

She's looking at my mouth. "I know. Me too."

She doesn't pull away when I lean in, and I think she might be leaning in a little too, so I press my mouth to the corner of hers, and it's like pressure's been building these past months, and finally just explodes in my chest as she lets her lips cover mine, soft and wet, and I'm ready to fall back onto the bed with her—but she pulls back. Smiles nervously, wipes her mouth.

"I'm sorry," she says, embarrassed. It's not pressure building in my chest now. It's dread. A whole lot of fucking dread. "I'm sorry—I shouldn't have done that."

"Shit." I stand up, ready to leave, because I can't sit here and pretend everything's okay anymore, like I'm not pissed she cheated on me, like I don't want to be with her.

"No—Nate, please don't go." She reaches for my hand, but when I pull away, she crosses her arms. "Stay. Let's talk about this."

Frustration leaks into my voice. "We've already talked about this."

She won't even look at me anymore. "I know. I love you, Nate. You know that I love you. But we have to stay—"

"Friends. Yeah. Right. Got it."

Flo lets out this sigh, and I know I'm being one of those

assholes who act like a dick when they don't get what they want, who they want. Fuck. I rub my head and mumble that I'm sorry. We're quiet for a while. I'm mad at myself. What did I think? That she was going to say that she still loves me? Say that she wants me to be her boyfriend again?

I sit down beside her. "Is it because of Lydia?" I ask, unable to look at her.

"It's not just because of Lydia. You and I are better as friends." When I don't answer, Flo suddenly says, "There has to be someone else that you like." She gets up, starts pacing the room, apparently super invested in my love life, maybe to make up for the fact that she isn't a part of it.

She glances at me as she walks by. "What about Ollie?"

I don't look at her. "What?"

"I mean—I don't know, there seemed to be something going on between you two."

Christ, it's like she can read my mind sometimes. No way in hell I'm admitting that I like Oliver James Hernández out loud, though. It'd be too complicated, telling the person I'm in love with that I have a crush on someone else. Besides, if I say it, Ollie will probably know by the end of the month, because Florence, bless her soul, doesn't always know when to keep her mouth shut.

And Ollie finding out? That'd inevitably mean the end of our friendship, one way or another. It doesn't matter what he may or may not have felt when we were kids. He has a boyfriend, and he's clearly not interested in me now.

I close my eyes, rub the palm of my hand across my face. "Nope. No, not really. I mean, there used to be a thing between us, sure—I had a stupid kid-crush on him."

She smiles like she's about to burst out laughing, but more in surprise than anything else. "Seriously? I was right?"

"Don't tell anyone," I say, pointing at her. "We're friends now. Nothing else. Trying to catch up after a few years. That's all."

She nods. "Okay, understood. But that doesn't help us figure out who you should date. Have you even *tried* liking someone else? What about Ashley? Not even as a joke. Seriously, why not Ash?"

"Because she's in love with Gideon?"

"I'm pretty sure Gideon's not into her."

"He doesn't even know."

"Oh, please—he just pretends not to know. Seriously, this could be really good for her. I'm going to set you guys up on a date," she says with the sort of finality I know better than to argue with. "And—you know, at least try to have a good time. You never know what'll happen," she says.

I hold in a sigh. Maybe she's right. Maybe this is the first step I need to take to get over her.

"All right. I'll try."

When I get home twenty minutes after seven, my mom is sitting on the couch, watching an episode of *Friends*. Again. I mean, I don't really self-identify as snarky or mean or anything, but for the love of God, doesn't anything else play on TV? (Okay. Maybe I'm a little snarky. I don't mean to be.)

"Nathan," she calls as soon as I step inside and kick off my shoes. I take a deep breath and try to prepare myself for the killing that's about to begin.

I pick up my Converses with my good hand and shuffle into the living room where she's spread out on the couch, her feet up on a cushion. She never really leaves that sofa. She works from home as a freelance copyeditor, and from the time I leave in the mornings until when I get home after school, she's always exactly where I left her on the couch.

She puts her laptop to the side now, looks me over. "How was your day?"

I glance at the air beside her. Is she trying to distract me so I won't see the killing coming? "It was fine."

"Rebecca told me that Oliver James is back home," she says.

"You spoke to Becca?"

"Yes—she's my daughter. We talk." She has an amused expression on her face. "Is that why you were out late yesterday?"

I cross my arms and shrug.

"You could've told me that. I would've made an exception."

But the point is that there shouldn't even have to be an exception in the first place. I'm sixteen, turning seventeen in

January. I'm going to leave for college in a couple of years. I should have a little more freedom.

I ask, "Does that mean I'm not grounded anymore?"

She purses her lips. "For now. But don't push me, Nate."

I nod and turn to leave before she can change her mind, but I don't get far. "How's Oliver?" she asks, sitting up on the sofa. "You should really bring him by. It's been years since we saw him."

"Yeah. Five years."

"You should bring him by," she says again.

I try to picture it: Ollie, sitting in the living room, being grilled by my mother as she asks all about Santa Fe and what his life plans are and how he's holding up here in Seattle. I can't think of anything I'd like to experience less.

"Sure," I say, turning away to escape to my bedroom.

"Want to eat dinner?" she calls after me. "I was thinking of ordering pizza."

"I'll just grab something later," I say over my shoulder. "I have a lot of homework."

She doesn't answer me, and I feel guilty—but now that Ollie has told me about that summer program, I want to try writing again. I haven't told my mom about the program. I know she'll just tell me that I can't apply. But if I apply and I *do* get accepted, that'd be pretty good ammunition to convince her to let me leave. If I apply and actually win first place with all costs covered, then maybe I wouldn't even need her permission.

I usually have to spend days revving up my nerve to write, but the deadline for the contest is only three months away, and some of the best scripts have taken years to complete. I get into my room and close the door, grab my laptop and flop onto my bed, open up my document and stare at the blank screen. Nothing's coming. Probably nothing ever will. I'll miss the deadline and watch Oliver James fly off to New York for the summer, leaving me behind with my depressed mother and a dream I'll never be brave enough to turn into a reality.

I roll onto my back and close my eyes. The key to brainstorming is to let my mind wander, right? My mind, as always, immediately jumps to Flo. I think about how we met. It was the first day of freshman year. Rebecca walked me to the courtyard, mussed up my hair, and told me she'd see me after school before heading inside for a student council meeting. I sat on a damp bench by myself, leg jiggling up and down as I watched the crowds of students laugh and hug and exchange photos of their summer vacations. A few kids from junior high were familiar, but it kind of seemed like everyone was already friends—and the only friend I'd ever had was Oliver James Hernández.

A girl with pink braids walked up to me. She stuck her hand out.

"I'm Florence Lim."

I wasn't really expecting anyone to talk to me. I looked around to see if she was talking to someone behind me, even though her hand was pointing directly at me. I took it hesitantly. "I'm—uh—Nathan Bird."

"Bird?" she said with a smile, plopping herself down on the bench next to me. "That's cute. I'm going to call you Bird. You can call me Florence. Or Flo. Either way, it doesn't matter." She unzipped her book bag and began to rummage for something.

"Oh. Okay."

"I saw you sitting by yourself, and figured we should be friends, since I don't know anyone else either. It sucks being a freshman, but it extra sucks being the new kid. I just moved here from Los Angeles," she said, looking at me from her bag as she pulled out a sketch pad and a pen. "I'm going to draw you, Bird."

"Oh. I—okay, sure."

"I'll be your friend," she said as she put the pen to paper, "but I'm not going to be your Manic Pixie Dream Girl, or pull you into some super-crazy life drama that ends in a road trip to South Carolina."

"Um. That's okay," I said, though I guess the road trip would've been nice.

She told me to sit still, so I did, and when she was finished, she ripped out the drawing from the sketch pad, and I saw a pretty good rendition of myself with scared eyes looking back at me. She smiled. "I'll let you have that one free of charge."

I look at my wall, where the drawing still hangs beside a movie poster of *The Godfather*. She was the first friend I'd had since Ollie, and I didn't want to lose her—but at night, in the dark with no one to judge me but myself, I messed up the sheets in Flo's honor. Though I guess she wouldn't feel too honored to know that. Especially when she told me she wanted to have sex at least a hundred times.

Why would I jerk off thinking about her, when I could actually be having sex with her? Was I too scared I'd somehow ruin our relationship? I wasn't sure how things were going to be different after we had sex—wasn't sure if she was going to stop loving me, or if I'd start to love her too much. There were too many questions. Too much about the whole idea of sex that scared the shit out of me.

Sex. With Flo. The thought gets stuck in my head like some song on repeat. I try to focus on writing, because that's what I want to do with my life: be a professional screenwriter, not a professional masturbator. But I can't concentrate, and finally I just give up and move my laptop and pull my sheets up over my head.

I feel guilty as all hell—and speaking of hell, I'm pretty sure there's a level reserved for ex-boyfriends jerking off to girls who said they want to be *friends*. I'm getting pretty into it when there's a knock on my door. I almost fall off my bed and yell that I'm coming (automatically wincing at the pun), and with my one good hand struggle to pull up my pants and smooth out my sheets and pump out a good amount of Purell that I keep on my desk for these special occasions. I get to the door in record time, open it expecting to see my mom, which would be the perfect mood killer—and instead get the opposite effect as I see Oliver James standing in front of me.

He signs a hello.

Asks if he can come in.

I glance behind me. Can Ollie tell I was just jerking off?

"Sorry," he says. "Your mom let me in. I tried texting, but you didn't answer, so I thought I'd just drop by—"

My phone's somewhere on my desk.

He moves his fist in a circle around his chest. "I could come back later."

Shit. I realize I'm being an asshole. "No—no, it's okay, come in."

I push the door open wider, and Oliver James steps past me and into my room.

8

OLIVER JAMES HASN'T BEEN IN MY BEDROOM IN FIVE YEARS.
The thought is jarring, somehow. Depressing, even. The realization that so much can change so easily. He walks in through
my doorway, staring around with big eyes, messing with the
end of his sweater. "Your room has changed a lot."

Not really. I've just collected a lot more crap. But I'm
getting the vibe that Ollie doesn't really want to chat about
that. I tap on his shoulder so that he turns around to look at
me. "Is everything okay?"

He shakes his head. "Not really. My parents are fighting.
Even being over a thousand miles apart can't really stop
them." His eyes are a little red, and his voice catches in a way
that lets me know he was just crying. Shit.

It's kind of funny. As much as Ollie won't force himself to laugh or smile, he's always been that much more open about crying. When we were kids, if anyone hurt his feelings, he wouldn't run away crying. He'd just sit right there, wiping his eyes until the tears stopped. It can make people uncomfortable sometimes—used to make me uncomfortable, too—but I understand it. Why fake an emotion and try to hide a real one?

He rolls his eyes at himself. "I should be used to this. I shouldn't have bothered you. It's just that I used to come over whenever they were fighting, so I figured—"

"No, it's okay." I sit down, wait for him to do the same. He looks uncomfortable on my bed. Maybe he can tell I was jerking off after all.

"It's just—we always talked about this kind of thing when we were younger, so I thought—"

"Yeah. No." I pick up my phone, typing quickly—I'm getting better at using it one-handed. I pass it to him. **You can talk to me about anything. You know, whenever.**

He points at himself, taps his head, points his index finger from the right side of his chest to the left, extends his thumb while shaking his head. "I know we're not as close as when we were kids."

I can't argue with that, even if I wish it weren't true. I shrug. **But I'd like to be again.**

He smiles a little—his first real smile since coming over. "My dad's an asshole," he says, shaking his head. "He wants me to move back to Santa Fe. Wants to take full custody.

96

There's no reason to. No point to do this. He's just trying to hurt my mom."

The thought of losing Ollie again makes my chest burn. But this isn't about me. I pinch my fingers together, point at him, bring my open palms toward myself, but I must have signed something incorrectly, because he squints at me, confused. "What do you want?" I ask him.

He shrugs. "I miss seeing Aiden every day. Miss my school, my friends. But it'd be unfair to just leave my mom. Dad's got his new girlfriend, and they're already talking about getting married, and he's thinking of having more kids—my mom only has me. I want to stay here. And, I mean, I know we're not as close as we used to be, but to lose you *again* for no reason but my dad's revenge . . ."

I can feel the emotion building in him. I put a hand on his shoulder, let it rub to his back, pull him closer and hide his face beneath my chin. He starts to just let it out, and I can feel the heat against my neck. We lie back on my bed, and I still kind of have a halfway hard-on, and it's really fucked up to be thinking this way when my ex–best friend/sort-of-best-friend-again is crying against me, but I want to press closer to him.

Ollie pulls away, wipes his face, but tears hang onto his lashes. His brown eyes meet mine, and he doesn't look away when I lean forward, when my mouth brushes his. We just stay like that, not moving, not breathing—until he pulls away, and I realize.

Oh my fucking God. I just kissed Ollie.

AGAIN.

We sit there. Both of us are stunned.

He opens his mouth to say something, but before anything comes out, my mom's calling my name. I jump off the bed and tell him that she's asking me to come downstairs, and I practically sprint out the door, almost tripping down the stairs.

My mom gives me a weird look. "Why're you running?"

Ollie's close behind, but when he stops beside me, she doesn't question his red face, thank God. Only asks the two of us to sit down and join her so that she can catch up with Ollie, ask him about Santa Fe. This is one of the times I gladly jump onto the couch beside her, but Oliver James apologizes and says that his own mom is expecting him.

"Maybe I can visit again another time," he says.

"That'd be great, Oliver James." She gives him a hug, says that it was nice to see him again, rolls her eyes when I barely raise my hand to wave goodbye. He ducks his head as he walks out the front door.

"I'll never understand boys and their need to *play it cool*," she says, sitting beside me.

I'm guessing there're a few things my mom wouldn't really understand.

At school the next morning, Flo is sitting with Gideon, Ash, and Oliver James on her favorite damp bench. They're all passing around Gideon's phone, laughing about something, as any group of friends normally would in any opening scene, and I know a script would have me walk up to them so that I could be filled in on the joke, and we'd all laugh together—but Ollie looks my way and his smile fades. I turn away and keep on walking right past them and through the door. Even across the courtyard, I can hear their laughter die down and feel their stares. I hear the slap of footsteps following me. It doesn't take long before Florence catches up with me in the hall, in front of my locker.

"Hey," she says.

"Hey."

She leans up against the lockers beside me. They're all a teal color, and the paint is peeling. "How's your morning going?"

I shrug and turn the lock to my numbers before popping it open.

"Are you mad or something?"

"No. Why would I be mad?" I chuck my books inside.

It's her turn to shrug now. "You're acting kind of weird."

"No, I'm not."

"Yeah. You're acting weird."

"I'm not acting weird, Flo."

She doesn't say anything else, and I guess that's the end of our conversation, but she keeps watching me.

And watches me during lunch, too, when Ollie tries to sit beside me in the greenhouse with a frown, looking like he wants to bring up yesterday, and I find an excuse to move to the other side of the bench, saying I want to stretch my legs. Florence sits down next to him instead, throwing me a *what the fuck is wrong with you?* glare, and begins to talk to him on her phone.

Ashley's noticed the exchange. "Nate, are you all right?" she asks. "You're really quiet today."

"I'm allowed to be quiet sometimes, right?"

"Yeah, but you're also being a dick about it," Gideon says, mouth full of pizza from the cafeteria.

I rub my temples with my middle fingers. He smiles.

"You can talk to us, you know," Ashley says.

I push away a pinch of annoyance. "I'm fine," I say, "except for feeling a little suffocated at the moment."

"You're a bad liar, Bird," Florence says without looking at me, typing and holding up her phone for Ollie to see. He laughs, nods. Flo glances at me. "It's not because of—you know, what happened with us last night, is it?"

This grabs Gideon and Ashley's attention. I try not to be too pissed about the fact that Flo has a tendency to bring up super-private things in front of other people. I shake my head. "No. I promise."

The bell rings, and I'm the first out of the greenhouse doors.

At the end of the day, Ollie sits by himself on the bench, waiting for me to walk back to our neighborhood, but I just pass right by him and keep going, even when I feel the heat of his stare on my back.

I can't face Oliver James. There's exactly one way a conversation about yesterday can end. Ollie might be super nice about it, but he'll tell me that he's with Aiden, and we need to stay friends. If he even says that at all. If he doesn't tell me to stay the hell away from him.

Shit. I can't believe I kissed him again.

I don't know what's going on with me, but until I figure it out, I think it's better to just stay away from Oliver James. Safer. Easier, not having to deal with the whys. Why I kissed him. Why I can't stop thinking about him, even as I'm thinking about Florence. Maybe staying away from him will help put things in perspective.

I walk to the fence where a line of bikes are chained and start fiddling with my lock. I see Florence walk up to me out of the corner of my eye, but ignore her as I struggle with the combination. I'm so ready for this cast to come off.

She leans against the fence, crossing her arms and eyeing me. "What's going on with you?"

The combination clicks—finally. "What do you mean?"

"Well, for one, you won't even look at me."

I stand straight and look at her. "Happy?"

"I could use a little less of the Nathan Bird attitude right now."

I sling my backpack over my shoulder. "Sorry."

She plays with one of her twists. "Are you all right? Did something happen?"

"No, nothing happened."

She doesn't believe me. "Ashley and I think you had a fight with Ollie."

My body involuntarily jolts. "Why would you think that?"

"Because you've been treating him like crap all day."

I swallow, then swing one leg over my bike. "I just need some space. There isn't anything wrong with that."

Florence stares at me. "Well, if you're treating him like shit just to get *some space*, I'd say yeah, there's something pretty wrong with that."

"Why do you even care so much?" I ask, but regret it the second I do.

Her face goes blank for a split second before she looks away, tucking a twist behind her ear. "I don't know. I guess I thought you were my best friend, and we talked to each other about everything."

I don't know how to respond to that, so I just tell her I have to head home. I push off and begin pedaling.

"Why the hell do you still ride that thing?" she says. "Your arm is *broken*."

I look over my shoulder. "I'll see you tomorrow."

And I think about Ollie the whole way home. The expression on his face, like I betrayed him somehow. That isn't fair either. We used to be best friends, but that was years ago.

He's only been back a few days. It shouldn't automatically be my responsibility to hang out with him again, right? I don't have to feel obligated to be his friend.

A small voice in me says that I'm just telling myself bullshit; and that might be true, but it's bullshit that makes me feel better. Everyone's allowed to lie to themselves every now and then.

Except that I still can't stop thinking about him. And that small voice tells me, maybe that's okay too.

9

DAYS PASS AND NOT MUCH CHANGES. I WAKE UP, EAT BREAK-
fast, go to school, scribble notes for my script in class, try not
to fall asleep in study hall, leave, and bike home—all while
avoiding the hell out of Oliver James. Ignoring him whenever he sits down in the greenhouse. Dodging him in between
classes. Making a break for it after school, before he can ask if
we can walk back to our neighborhood together. Ignoring the
text messages he sends, first asking if we can hang out. Second
asking if he's done something wrong. Third apologizing for
what happened.

Ignoring him kind of started out as being the easy thing
to do—just a break, while I tried to figure myself out. But
now it's gotten too weird. Even if I want to hang out with him

again (which I'm still not 100 percent sure about anyway), it's almost too late to go back now. It was only at a level-20 awkward before, but now the building silence has helped the awkwardness reach a level-100.

I'm sitting in the greenhouse during free period, trying to write down ideas for my script. I've decided I'm not going to apply to the Emerging Creatives contest anymore. If Ollie and I both get in, that wouldn't exactly be a fun summer in New York. But I still want to write—still want to finish my first script. I'm about to finish outlining a scene when the door swings open and Ashley walks in. She smiles, sits down across from me, and pulls out a notebook also. "Free period?"

I nod.

"Me too. Is it okay if I sit with you?"

I'm not sure why it wouldn't be. "Yeah, of course."

We're quiet for a long while, me scribbling notes and trying to concentrate—but it's a little harder now with Ashley there. She keeps glancing up at me, like she wants to say something, and I wish to God she'd just say it—until finally she takes a deep breath.

"Florence spoke to me, you know," she says. "Apparently she wants us to go on a date."

Shit. I'd somehow forgotten all about that, what with kissing both my current and former best friends. "Uh. Okay."

She plays with the ends of her hair, maybe a little embarrassed also. "It's okay if you don't want to."

I force myself to remember why I agreed to it. Flo's right. I have to get myself out there if I want to get over her—and Ollie. "No." Her face drops. "No, I mean—yeah, no, I want to."

Ash smiles as if she's relieved. It's a nice reminder that I'm not the only person around with a fear of rejection. "How about tonight?"

"Sure. I just have to be home by seven." I internally strangle myself. "In, you know, the coolest way possible."

She laughs. "Don't worry, I probably shouldn't stay out too late anyway." The bell rings. We start to pack up our backpacks and head to the AP English class we have together. Ollie is across the courtyard. He hasn't seen me, so I duck my head and hurry in the opposite direction.

Flo and I never once went on a date. We started hanging out as friends. We'd walk around downtown as friends. And then we started kissing as friends. And then we started kissing as boyfriend and girlfriend. But we never once said that we'd go somewhere romantic and call it a *date*.

"Why is that?" Flo asked one night. Doors closed, lights off, Ethel curled up on her favorite pillow, the glow of a laptop screen making Florence's eyes shine. We hadn't really been watching the movie. Our shirts were on the floor.

"Why is what?"

"Why haven't we gone out on a date yet?"

I shrugged. "I dunno."

"Impressive answer, Bird."

"What? I mean—what do you want me to say?"

"Why're you getting so defensive?"

"I'm not getting defensive." I was getting pretty defensive. She was quiet. "I mean. It's not like I don't think you're not worth a date or something. Of course you're worth a date."

"Yes. I know that."

"But I mean—we don't really have to, right? I feel like it's a little . . . I don't know. Corny, I guess. We don't need to do that, to know that we like each other." By that point, I was pretty sure I was in love with her, but I wasn't about to say it out loud.

She sat up. "Sure, it's corny . . . but it's still nice. It's okay to show affection."

"I know that."

"You can be emotionally unavailable sometimes."

"Oh. Wow. Okay. Should I just go, or—"

"I'm just saying—it's like you don't want me to know that you like me."

"I'm confused."

"You're acting like it's wrong, somehow, to actually like someone. Maybe even love them."

Was she onto me? I couldn't take that conversation. Suddenly, I just really wanted to watch the movie. Truman raced into the woods with the power plant guys chasing after him. I didn't say anything. I could see her shaking her head in the dark.

"It's okay to love someone."

"I know that." I didn't know that. I still don't think I do. It's a little like voluntarily standing in front of a firing squad. Opening myself up to be hurt, since I know hurt is inevitable.

Flo didn't say anything else. We sat there in quiet for a long time. I was afraid to speak. She'd hear my voice breaking. My breath was too ragged. I forced myself to say something. "I just don't want to get hurt."

She frowned. "No one wants to be hurt. No one wants to risk that. But if we don't risk it . . . then we don't give ourselves the chance to fall in love. Then we don't have anything."

I don't really know what's worse: living without love so that you don't get hurt, or getting hurt repeatedly in an attempt to find it.

Ashley doesn't like how society expects guys to choose restaurants and pay for everything, so she takes me to a vegetarian café where the mugs are tiny and porcelain and little hearts are designed into the lattes. We try to have a normal conversation, awkwardly fumbling for topics to distract us from the weirdness of the situation. ("Played the new *Mass Effect* yet?" "Nope. The husks freak me out too much. Watched the new Guillermo del Toro yet?" "No. But I watched *Zootopia*. That was pretty good.")

After a long silence, Ash takes a sip from her latte. "So," she says, "Florence tells me you're a virgin."

I almost spit hot chocolate on her. "She told you *what*?"

"Oh," Ash says, "it's not true?"

I put my face down into my hand, then place my chin into my palm and just smile. "Yeah. Yeah, it's true."

"It's nothing to be embarrassed about," she says earnestly, reaching across the table to grab my hand—the hand of my broken arm. I flinch, but she doesn't notice as she squeezes tighter. "We all start out as virgins."

I laugh a little. She smiles, then takes another sip. "I lied, you know."

"Lied?"

She nods, not looking at me. "I'm a virgin, too. I don't even know why I said I wasn't. It was so stupid."

I'm not sure what to say. "Uh. I guess there's all this pressure to, you know, have sex."

She shrugs, staring down at her latte.

I guess it's my turn to say something. "Sorry—this is kind of weird."

"I know," she says. "I've never really thought of you as anything but a friend. A really cute friend, though, I have to admit," she adds with a smile.

I can't help but feel a small sting of rejection. "Did you tell that to Flo?"

"Yeah, but I also thought it'd be nice to try going out with you anyway. I mean, why not?" She takes another sip before putting the mug down with a tiny clatter. "I'm sick and tired of looking around at everyone else falling in love, and telling myself that I don't deserve it, too. But I have to get myself out there if I want it to happen, right?" She hesitates. "And, you know—I've been thinking—if you want to try having sex . . . Maybe we could be each other's firsts. Just to get it over with."

I shift in my chair, carefully, so she can't tell I'm trying to adjust my pants, because yes, I am the pathetic sort of guy that gets a boner just at the suggestion of having sex. "That's—nice of you, Ash, but you don't have to do that."

"I know," she says. "Of course I don't have to. But I want to. I wouldn't mind it with you, anyway. It's not like we have to be *in love*. I like you, and respect you, and think you're cute. If you like me, respect me, and think I'm cute too—then, why not?"

I swallow and try to act as blasé about it as Ashley is, but I must not be doing a good job of it, because she frowns as she watches me.

"I—uh—guess I kind of do want my first time to be with someone I love," I say.

She bites her lip. "Is there someone you're in love with now?" When I don't answer, she adds, "Flo said you might still be a little hung up on her."

"Jesus Christ. I'm not *hung up* on Florence. She says she wants to stay friends, and she's going out with Lydia now—so I'm moving on."

Ashley clearly doesn't believe me. With reason. "Then why not? We could make a date of it. This weekend, you could come over to my place. My parents are out of town for a week."

I'll give Ash one thing: she really doesn't back down when she wants something. "Well—I mean, I guess I do like someone else."

Her eyes widen. Florence didn't brief her on this possibility. "Really? Who?"

"It's no one."

"It's clearly someone. Who is it?"

I shake my head. "Really. I can't tell you. It's a little embarrassing."

I think she's more disappointed I won't tell her who I have a crush on than by the fact that I won't have sex with her, but she finally lets it go as we agree we won't be doing the dirty any time soon.

"Why do you want to have sex so badly anyway?" I ask, embarrassed to even be on this topic with Ashley—but she's surprisingly more mature about it than I am.

She shrugs. "I guess there's someone I like too," she says, not looking at me, "and I think that he prefers people who are . . . experienced."

I want to ask Ashley where she got that idea—it isn't like Gideon's said he refuses to date virgins, or even that sex is actually important to him. But that would require me revealing I know who she likes, and if she were ready to tell me that, she would've said it herself.

"I think the right person for you wouldn't care about something like that," I tell her.

She gives me a small smile. "You might be right."

Ashley lives close to Capitol Hill, so on her way to the bus, we take a walk by the regular tourist spots—Pike, the Needle. It's a nice enough day to enjoy the peeks of sunlight shining through the gray clouds, and I have to admit, I like spending time with Ash. We usually only hang out in the greenhouse during lunch, and before and after school in the courtyard, so this is a nice change.

We're passing by a comic book and video game store when Ash grabs my arm (the unbroken one, thank God). "Look— isn't that Flo?"

Florence walks out of the store right ahead of us, face turned toward Gideon—and Ollie. My heart drops. This is too much of a coincidence. They had to have planned this.

Flo swings her head around with this overexaggerated look of surprise on her face. She grins as we walk closer. "Oh, hey—it's the lovebirds."

Gideon throws an arm around my shoulder. "How was the date?" he asks.

"Uh." I look at Ashley, and see a flicker of hurt at the fact that Gideon so obviously couldn't care less if she's going out with anyone else—but she recovers quickly.

"It was great," Ashley says. She leans closer to me, snuggling my unbroken arm. "Bird and I decided we're better off as friends."

Ash loops her arm with Florence's as they walk off in front of us, chatting away—most likely about every single thing I'd done and said while on our date. Gideon trails behind them. Oliver stands like he's stuck in cement, peering at me through his eyelashes. He signs a hello. I sign a hello back.

He begins to walk beside me, and I try to see if there's a way for me to speed up and join Gideon, strike up a convo that'd leave Oliver James in the dust (because I'm a shitty person, and that's the kind of thing shitty people do).

I'm walking pretty fast, but Oliver has no trouble keeping up. When'd his legs get so freaking long?

"It's been a while," he says out loud. I notice Florence and Ashley glancing over their shoulders at us.

I nod. "Yeah." Almost a week since whatever-the-hell-that-was transpired in my room. Almost a week of avoiding Oliver James.

"I texted," he says, and I wish he'd just sign or something, because now Gideon's trailing behind a little too much, walking practically right beside him. Ollie doesn't seem to notice—he's just staring at his feet while he walks, glancing up at me with those damn eyes.

"Yeah. Sorry." I scratch my arm.

"Look," he says, slowing to a stop, and ahead of us the

others turn around. "If you don't want to be friends with me or—or hang around me anymore, it's fine. I get it." He can't look at me while he speaks. "I just kind of need you to say it, or I won't know if I should just leave you alone or . . ."

I'm quiet. The others are watching. I shrug. "Yeah. I mean, I guess it'd be nice to have some space."

No one says a word. Oliver isn't staring at his feet anymore—he's looking up at me with this surprised, hurt look.

"Not to be an asshole," I say quickly, even though that's exactly what I'm being, "I just—yeah, I mean, I have the friends I need, you know?"

Ollie nods slowly.

"On second thought, I think I'm just going to head home," I say, walking backward. "See you guys later, all right?"

No one says goodbye as they watch me leave. Not that I can blame them. I know it was a shitty thing to do. But I'd rather hurt Ollie first, before he hurts me. That's what's most fucked up of all.

When I get home, I decide to try to write my script again—get my mind off the fuckery that is currently my life. I think about that Emerging Creatives program. Even though I'd already decided not to apply, I feel a heaviness knowing I couldn't now even if I wanted to. I'm an asshole, but not such an asshole that I'd treat the guy like shit and then apply to the contest he told me about. Besides, there isn't a chance in hell that I'd actually win, so there's no point in applying. I just want to finish my first script—but after everything that's happened, I'm too distracted, and absolutely nothing's coming to me.

I'm in the middle of "writing" (by which I actually mean staring at the screen) when I get an invitation to video chat with Rebecca. If I don't answer, I know she'll flip out at me—she's pretty similar to our mom in that way—so I sigh and click accept.

"Hey, Becca," I say, sitting up. "How's life?"

She waves at the screen. "Pretty okay. College party life just isn't what I thought it'd be—but maybe that's because I'm not actually going to any parties."

"Why aren't you going to any parties?"

"Because there isn't any time!" She covers her face with her hands. "Exams are killing me. I'm starting to question a psychology major."

"Really?"

"Nah, I guess not. It's just easy to feel that way now when I'm stressed." She leans out of the screen for a second, and something out of view clatters. "What's going on with you?"

I say the first thing that comes to mind. "Well, I went on a date with Ashley."

She frowns at the screen. "Who?"

It's a nice reminder that not everything revolves around the drama of my life. "You know, Ashley Perkins? She hangs out with me, Florence, and Gideon."

"Oh," she says, but it's clear she has no idea who I'm talking about. "How'd it go?"

"We decided we were better off as friends."

She nods slowly, watching me carefully. "You seem pretty bummed."

"I am, I guess, but not about that." I hesitate. A part of me wants to tell Becca everything, but I'm not even sure where to begin.

She sees the expression on my face. "Problems with Florence again? Is she still dating that girl? What was her name?"

"Lydia," I say, "and no, actually, for once it doesn't have anything to do with her." I tell her what happened this afternoon with Ollie, cringing a little as I recount what I did and said—but careful not to even hint to what'd happened in my bedroom a week before.

I just want to hear someone tell me that what I said to Ollie isn't as bad as I think, but I should've known better with my sister. She jumps into psychotherapy mode. "Well, why'd you tell him that?"

I shrug. "I just want some space."

"From what?"

"I don't know. I was feeling this pressure, I guess, to be his friend."

She narrows her eyes at me. "You're lying."

My heart jumps a beat. "No, I'm not."

"I know you too well, Nate," she says. "You never feel pressured into anything."

"That's not true."

She looks a little hurt now, I guess because I'm not opening up to her. We're always honest with each other. "It sounds to me like you're not treating Oliver James well because of some underlying fears or insecurities."

My leg begins to jiggle and I look away from the laptop. I never should've answered the video chat invitation.

"Is it Flo? Are you afraid of making her jealous, because Oliver James used to be your best friend?"

"No."

"Is it Ollie? Are you afraid of getting close, only for him to leave again?"

"Would you stop psychoanalyzing everything?"

She's really watching me closely now. I try not to blink or do anything that signals I'm nervous or lying, but I don't think it's working.

"You mentioned this date with Ashley," she says. "Why'd you decide you were better off as friends?"

I shrug. "What does that have to do with Oliver James?"

She doesn't take the bait. "And you still have feelings for Florence, right?"

"Of course I do. We went out for a year."

She pauses. "How do you feel about Ollie?" she asks.

"What do you mean?"

"I mean, is he still pretty much the same guy as when you were eleven?"

"Yeah, I guess. Pretty much."

She's frowning. "Have you been—I don't know, feeling any differently toward him?"

I blink too many times. "Different how?"

"Like. I don't know." Now she's having a hard time looking at the screen. "You guys were really close when you were little, and I always wondered . . . do you have a crush on him?"

"Christ, Becca."

She doesn't answer me. Just waits for me to respond. And when I can't think of anything to say, only feel myself getting hot with embarrassment, the silence stretches on longer than I can take and I exit the hell out of the video chat and slam my laptop shut and try not to cry, because that would be an amazingly new level of pathetic that I'm just not ready to reach yet.

My cell phone begins to buzz. I press ignore. I get a text from Becca, and three others almost simultaneously. I put my phone on silent. There's a knock on my door. My mom opens it, holding out her phone.

"Nate, it's your sister—she says she needs to speak to you."

I could fucking scream. I get up, grab the phone, and almost end the call—but with our mom watching, I close my eyes and put it to my ear.

"Nate?" Becca says. Her voice is softer than it usually is.

"Yeah, I'm here."

"You know I love you, right?"

I look at my mom, who's still watching me curiously. I turn my back to her. "Yeah."

"Whether you have a thing for Flo or Ollie—it doesn't matter to me. You know that."

"Okay."

"I love you, little brother."

"I know."

"Don't Han Solo me."

"Okay. I love you too."

"You need to tell him."

"What?"

"You need to tell Ollie. You can't just avoid him. From what you told me, it sounds like you're pushing him away because you're afraid of what he'd do or say if he found out how you feel. But you're only hurting him, and you're hurting yourself."

"I can't tell him something like that."

My mom taps my shoulder and reaches out for the phone. "You have your own," she says pointedly. I nod and tell Becca I have to go, then hand the phone to my mom.

"Everything okay?" she asks with some concern. I know I'm lucky to have a mom who actually gives a shit.

"Yeah," I lie, then shake my head. "I don't know. Not really. But I'll be all right."

She frowns now, crosses her arms. "Anything you want to talk about?" she asks. "I know I'm not sixteen anymore, but I might be able to give you some advice."

I shrug. "Thanks—but I think this is one I have to figure out on my own."

"Okay." She tugs on one of my curls. "Just say the word if you want to talk."

10

I'M SITTING ALONE AT LUNCH, OUT IN THE COURTYARD, trying to get through some homework I didn't feel like finishing last night, not paying attention to anything or anyone but myself, so I'm surprised when Florence comes out of nowhere and sits down beside me. As soon as she appears, I realize I'm on her favorite bench. I wonder if she thinks I was secretly trying to get her to come sit with me. Maybe I subconsciously was.

"Bird," she says, nodding her head formally.

"Lim," I say, though it sounds more like a question.

I try to act like I don't give a crap that she's here—but my heart starts hammering in my chest. I've missed her. I'm still in love with her, I know that I am—even if I've got feelings for Ollie too. Having feelings for one person doesn't automatically cancel out feelings I have for another.

Flo and I just keep looking at each other. Neither of us speaking. It's awkward as fuck.

"You're an idiot," she says. "You know that, right?"

I take a breath. "Yeah, I know."

"What's going on with you? Ollie wouldn't say what happened, but he thought he did something to piss you off. *Did he do something?*"

Instant image of Ollie doing something to me. Probably not what Flo had in mind. I shake my head. "Nope."

She squints at me. "Ash and I have some theories."

"Uh. Okay. What're the theories?"

"That you're lonely and sad but don't want to talk about it," Flo says.

"Wow. I mean, that makes me sound pathetic."

"Well, maybe you are, Nate," Florence says. "Have you ever thought of that?"

"Yeah. Pretty much every day."

She rolls her eyes. "Don't try to guilt trip me."

"I'm not trying to guilt trip you," I say. She watches me with a blank stare. "Okay. All right. I'm sorry."

"Apology accepted," she says. "We think you must be struggling with something, even though you won't say what it is, and that's why you freaked out on Ollie."

I try not to let anything show. Like Florence will immediately figure out that I've got a thing for Oliver James just by looking at my face. I don't think I can take anyone else

122

knowing my deepest, darkest secret yet. Especially not her. "I guess."

"I'm not going to pressure you into saying something you don't want to say," she says. "But you should come sit with us."

I think of Ollie, Ash, and Gideon, watching me as I return like the prodigal son. The silence as I sit down, no one really knowing what to say. Having to publicly apologize to Oliver James. "That's okay."

"Oh, come on."

"No, really—I mean, maybe tomorrow," I say. "Lunch is almost over now anyway."

She narrows her eyes at me. "Fine. But let's hang out after school. How about Sun Bird Comics?"

There's a reason I fell in love with Flo. She's incredible. I mean, not many people would be so forgiving or empathetic without demanding to know why I was acting like such a piece of shit. "Yeah, we haven't been there in a while."

And then she says: "Okay—Lydia's meeting me there, too." She must see my face drop. "That's okay, right?"

I haven't had the heart to tell Florence that not only do I dislike Lydia as a person, but I'm only pretending to be over the fact that Flo left me for her—cheated on me with her. I try not to think about it a lot, because I decided to forgive Florence—but that doesn't mean I have to forgive Lydia, too.

"Uh. Yeah." I force a smile. "That's fine."

Sun Bird Comics is a shop over on Capitol Hill. I used to follow Flo to work when she had her summer job . . . But now, all I can wonder is exactly what happened between Florence and Lydia. What did Lydia say to make Florence like her? Were they flirting over *X-Men* comics? Bantering behind the register? I pick up *Watchmen*, since I thought the movie was pretty good. Flo heads straight for the Marvel section, and we occupy a corner of the rough gray carpet, knees bumping into each other, as we wait for Lydia.

"Are you sure you're okay with this?" Flo asks, looking up at me from the latest *Miss America*, Florence's newest obsession. "I mean—I'd really like it if we could all hang out and be friends, but if you're not comfortable with it . . ."

I'm not comfortable with it. I know I'm not. But my illogical mind thinks that if Florence sees how forgiving I am, then maybe she'll see what a great boyfriend I was, and maybe she'll want me back. I ignore the part of my brain that tells me this makes absolutely no sense.

I start to say I'm fine, when Lydia rounds the corner. Florence's face lights up and she jumps to her feet and stretches out her arms for a hug. "Hey, Lyds," she says, and Lydia grins, puts her arms around Florence's waist, and kisses her. I become super interested in the copy of *Watchmen* I'm holding.

They pull away. "Hey, Nate," Lydia says, and I can see some hesitation in her eyes. She probably sees me as the ex-boyfriend that won't go away and crashed her date with

Florence. I guess that's pretty much what I am. She sits down on Florence's other side, hand on Flo's knee. Her hair's dyed green today, and she has on a Nine Inch Nails hoodie.

"You weren't waiting long, were you?" Lydia asks Flo.

Florence slips her hand into Lydia's. "No, just a few minutes."

"Which issue is that?"

They begin to talk about *Miss America* and Gabby Rivera and Florence's plans to write and illustrate her own series, and Lydia says that's awesome and kisses Flo's cheek, then her mouth, and I'm officially living every third wheel's worst nightmare.

Florence clears her throat, glancing at me and wiping her lips like she's realized that it might be a little shitty to kiss Lydia in front of me. "I'm going to look for the new *Black Panther*," she says, then gives Lydia a pointed look as she gets up, which isn't weird at all.

We sit there with a Flo-sized gap between us. Lydia's not looking at me, but she says, "So," then pauses, obviously struggling for a topic to talk about. She nods her head at the *Watchmen* in my hands. "Liking that so far?"

"Uh—yeah. It's pretty similar to the movie, and the movie was good, so . . ."

She nods slowly, like she couldn't possibly be more bored out of her mind. "Listen," she says, "I'm just going to be frank. I like Florence a lot, and she asked me to try being your friend, so can we just agree to tell her we had a great conversation about—I don't know, movies made from comics?"

This is one of the many times Lydia's personality has rubbed me the wrong way. "Yeah. Sure, I guess."

She picks up the copy of *Miss America* Florence left behind, and I pretend I'm reading through *Watchmen* also, but I'm too distracted to focus on the words. I want to ask Lydia what it is, besides her coolness factor, that Florence likes so much more. What made her choose Lydia over me? Was she just bored with me? Did she want to date someone who was into comics also? Was it because I was too afraid to have sex with her? (Okay, maybe I wouldn't ask Lydia that one.)

I remember what Florence said the night she admitted she'd cheated on me. Flo and Lydia had both been working here at Sun Bird Comics part-time and quickly became friends. Flo admitted she'd started to get a crush a couple of weeks before anything happened, but one night Lydia was walking her to the bus stop, and she kissed Florence. Florence kissed back. It was just a kiss, but it was enough. Flo took the bus to my neighborhood, knocked on my door crying, and said that we should break up.

"You know," Lydia says, slapping the comic closed, "I don't know what you're trying to do."

I frown. "What do you mean?"

"Coming here, hanging out. Are you trying to make me feel bad or something?"

"No," I say, a little more loudly than I mean to. "Flo asked me to come here. You said it yourself. She wants us to be friends. But I mean," I add, "if you do feel bad, I wouldn't blame you."

She narrows her eyes. "Oh, fuck off. Why the hell would I feel bad?"

"Maybe because you kissed Flo, knowing she had a boyfriend?"

"No, I kissed Flo knowing that she wanted me to."

I don't have a quick enough comeback for that one.

"She broke up with you. She's with me. Get over it, and stop obsessing over my girlfriend."

"I'm not *obsessing* over her," I say, even though I am.

Lydia gives me a skeptical look. "I don't buy that you're just back to being Flo's best friend."

"What, afraid that she'll want to be with me again?" I ask.

She smiles at me. "Not really."

I'm tempted to tell her that Flo and I kissed. It was just for a split second, and Florence stopped us just as we started, but it was still a kiss, and it would still hurt Lydia just as much as she's hurting me. But it's not my place to say. And I wouldn't get Florence back just because I got her in trouble with Lydia.

Florence comes back with a stack of comics in her hands. They almost topple over as she reclaims her seat in between us. "I'm back," she says in a singsong voice. She grins at me. "What'd you guys talk about?"

I close *Watchmen* and abandon it on the floor. "I'm going home," I say.

"Wait, what?" Florence says.

I head for the door, but Flo follows me outside onto the sidewalk, nearly knocking into a couple walking hand in hand. She grabs my elbow. "Is everything all right?"

How do I say that her girlfriend is an asshole without coming across like a jealous ex? Besides, maybe Lydia was right about some things—maybe I am obsessing over Florence, when I know she's already moved on. "I guess I just realized it's a little weird after all," I say, "hanging out with you and Lydia."

She looks surprised, then hurt, then worried all at once. "Okay. I mean—I get it, I understand. I just kind of hoped we could all—I don't know, be friends."

"Is that because you actually want me and Lydia to be friends," I ask, "or is that because you want to feel better about cheating on me?"

She looks more hurt than anything else now. She opens her mouth, closes it again.

"Sorry." I rub the back of my neck.

"No—I mean, maybe you're right. Maybe I'm just trying to make myself feel better." She can't look at me. I want to wrap my arms around her, the same way that Lydia did. But I can't. It's time to get used to that.

"Why her?" I ask.

She looks up, confused.

"Why Lydia over me?"

Florence pulls on one of her twists. "It's not like I *chose* her instead of you," she says. "I just fell in love with her, is all." She sees my face, takes my hand. I want to squeeze hers and pull away simultaneously, and I'm not really sure which I should do. "I love you," she says. "You know that, right?"

"Yeah," I say. "But just as friends."

"Doesn't mean I love you any less."

I'm not really sure what to say—not too sure how I'm feeling, either—so I tell Florence that I'll see her tomorrow. I pull my hand away from hers, a little harder than I mean to, making her flinch. She doesn't try to stop me as I head to the bus stop.

11

WHEN I WALK THROUGH THE FRONT DOOR, KICKING OFF MY Converse sneakers and bending over to pick them up, my mom's standing at the kitchen counter. She turns over a newspaper as she glances up at me over the rims of her reading glasses. She checks her wristwatch.

"Hey, Mom," I say, walking into the kitchen, shoes in my hand.

"Why so early?" she asks, looking back to the newspaper on the counter. "It's not even five yet."

I lean against the counter. "I realized that this is my junior year, and I really need to take my future more seriously."

She makes a face. "When did my son become so funny?"

"I was born this way."

She folds the newspaper, slides off her glasses. "I was thinking of ordering a pizza. What kind do you want?"

"Pepperoni."

"So boring."

I watch as she picks up her phone to call in an order of half pepperoni, half pineapple, sausage, onions, and peppers. She puts the phone back down and glances at me with a growing smile. "What is it? I've never seen you look so pensive."

"What do you mean? I'm always pensive."

She raises an eyebrow. "If you say so."

She keeps watching me, question lingering. I'm not sure if I want to tell my mom—I kind of like that she's the one last person that remembers who Florence and I used to be, before this summer, before Flo's mistake—but I'm also starting to realize that there isn't any point to holding on to our relationship of the past.

"You know how Flo and I broke up, right?" I ask.

She quirks her head to the side, smile gone. "Yeah."

"Well," I say, swallowing and looking up at her, "she kind of cheated on me."

My mom's eyes widen. "What?"

"Yeah—she cheated on me with her coworker at Sun Bird Comics this summer."

"I can't believe that," she says. "Florence was always so nice."

I shrug. "She's still nice. She just made a mistake, I guess."

She's frowning, arms crossed. "Are you all right?"

"It's been a few months now."

"That doesn't answer my question."

I let out a quick sigh. "I mean—I guess. I don't know?"

She leans on her elbows on the countertop. "It's okay if you're still upset about it. That's not something many people easily get over."

"I just keep wondering *why*, you know?"

"I'm sure you did nothing wrong. She's the one who made a mistake, Nate. You're perfect exactly the way you are, and when it's meant to be, you'll find someone who's perfect for you."

I ignore the feeling that she couldn't be more wrong. "You're my mom. You have to say that."

"Yes, but mothers are also always right." We stand quietly for a while. "I can't believe her," she says. "If I'd known, I never would've let Florence come over."

I try not to laugh. "She's still my best friend."

She smiles, reaches out to ruffle my curls, mutters something about my hair growing fast. "I have something to run by you," she says.

"Okay."

"I was thinking about what you said, about living my life . . ."

I cringe. "Sorry."

"Well, I didn't like the way you said it, but you were

right," she says, nodding. "I'm thinking of starting to date again."

"Date?" I repeat.

"Yeah, date," she says with amusement in her voice. "You know, that thing people do when they want to—"

"Okay, yeah, I got it."

I'm not sure how to feel. First, I'm a little grossed out at the thought of my mom dating. Second, I feel a little betrayed, I guess, that she'd want to meet other people—as if my dad's someone to move on from, to forget about. Third, and finally . . . I'm surprised that she's even willing to try again.

"What do you think?" she asks.

I shrug. "Aren't you afraid of—I don't know . . ."

She crosses her arms. "Finding someone new, just to lose them again?" she asks.

I nod.

She sighs. "Sure. That's always a risk, right?" she says. "But with your dad, it was a risk worth taking."

I'm not so sure—not sure it'd ever be worth it. Falling for the love of your life while knowing that you will lose them. Even if it does work out, and they're together for the rest of their lives, neither can live forever. All relationships end in heartbreak and tragedy eventually.

But I can tell my mom wants me to say I'm okay with it, so that's what I tell her. She smiles and pats my cheek, and we move into the living room to wait for the pizza.

* * *

It's the weekend, which is weird, because usually I'd spend my Saturdays over at Florence's, or downtown with her or Gideon—but things have been a little awkward since I met up with Flo and Lydia. I think she's waiting for me to text her, to let her know I'm not angry anymore. Problem is, I'm still pretty mad. It's like all the anger I hid away for the past few months is forcing its way to the surface.

I take a bus by myself, passing Pike and the Space Needle and all of the other regular tourist spots, before getting off on Cherry Street. It's a brighter, sunnier day than usual, so the sidewalks are crowded with tourists and locals alike, hanging on corners, laughing, holding hands, carrying shopping bags, taking pictures. I turn a corner and head into Sparrow & Nightingale, cold air blasting, which is a relief after the heat outside. This is Florence's favorite spot. She introduced it to me when we first met, before we decided to become boyfriend and girlfriend. I guess it's even stranger being here without her, but maybe I really do need some space to figure some things out. Maybe I'm not as okay with her cheating on me as I wanted to be.

Sparrow & Nightingale is a pretty amazing place. The store is broken into different collections: vintage clothes in one section, VHS tapes and vinyl records in another, first editions of books locked away in glass cases. I'm heading for the VHS section when I see a tangle of familiar curls, a pair of dimples—Oliver James. He's seen me, too, but he looks away the second I catch him staring.

We haven't spoken in days—not since I was an asshole to him after my date with Ashley. I think about how it felt, being on the receiving end of bullshit from Lydia. I shouldn't have said what I did, I already know that.

I walk up to him hesitantly, and he sees me coming—puts back a book of photography on its shelf, takes a big breath.

I sign a hello with a half smile. "Following me now?" He only stares at me, so I add, "Joking. It was just a bad joke."

He holds up his palms as if carrying something, moves them in and out. "What do you want?"

That's a fair response, I guess, after the way I treated him.

"I—uh—wasn't expecting to see you here."

He narrows his eyes at me, and I can tell he didn't understand what I said, which just makes him more frustrated.

I don't know how to sign what I told him, so I pull out my phone, type quickly, hand it to him.

He lets out an impatient breath, hands the phone back to me. "Florence told me about this place, so I decided to check it out."

"Oh," I say, craning my neck around. I fingerspell F-L-O, turn my palms upward and move them in circles.

"No," he says flatly. "She's on a date with Lydia."

I clench my jaw, nod.

"I should get going," he says, turning his back on me—I

reach out for his arm, but he yanks it away at the last second.

"Sorry," I say quickly. "I—I wanted to say sorry for what I said to you the other day. It was stupid. I was just embarrassed about—" I can't even say it. Warmth creeps up my neck. I clear my throat. "You know."

He's watching, waiting. His blank expression makes it impossible to know if he understands what I'm saying or not. If he cares or not.

"I was thinking—maybe we could start over. Try being friends again."

"Friends don't treat each other like shit," he says.

I bite my lip, look away. "I know."

"I don't like being spoken to that way," he says, his voice getting louder.

"I know. I'm sorry."

"That's the way my dad speaks to my mom," he says. "Don't talk to me that way ever again."

Shit. "You're right. I promise I won't."

He doesn't speak for a second—just watches me like he's trying to figure out if he can believe me or not, if he can really trust me again. "We can try," he says. "But if something's going on with you—just talk to me. We always used to just talk to each other instead of . . ."

"Instead of being assholes?" I offer.

He clenches his jaw, nods.

"Yeah, I—" I hesitate. "I don't know what the hell that was. I'm sorry. I really am."

He lets out a breath and picks up another book of photography—this time by Sally Mann—and begins to flip through the pages.

He doesn't look at me as he says, "I really like this place a lot."

I can't help but grin, wiping my hands on my jeans. "Yeah." I type quickly, hold out the phone to him. He doesn't take it, but his eyes skim. **Flo and I used to come here a lot when we were going out.**

He glances up at me. "I didn't know you two dated."

"She didn't tell you?"

"No, she didn't." He puts the book down.

It was for a year.

He nods, and I can tell he's still struggling to forgive me, to move on. I can't really blame him.

He turns to me. "I never asked you. How'd your talk with Ashley go? You know, when she asked if I was interested? She's been acting like everything's fine. She hasn't brought it up, anyway."

I grimace at the memory. **You're already breaking hearts.**

"Oh, come on," he says, genuinely grinning—but then his grin begins to fade. "You don't really think she's heartbroken, do you?"

I laugh and shake my head.

He puts his knuckles together, turns them over with the thumbs up, and points at me.

I put the back of my right hand into my left palm, because

there's really nothing else I can say to that question.

He hesitates, then asks, "Did I do something wrong? Is that why you freaked out on me? Maybe I shouldn't have come over. We're not as close as when we were kids."

Even when he's upset, the corners of his lips are turned up naturally in this cute, I'd-kind-of-like-to-kiss-the-corners-of-your-mouth way. I extend my thumb from my chin, shaking my head, put one hand in a fist in front of my chest and use my other hand to point at him. "It's not your fault." I steal Florence and Ashley's official diagnosis. "I'm just going through something."

Ollie frowns. "Is there anything I can do to help?"

I have to look away from his mouth. I'm not reading lips. There's no reason for me to be staring at his mouth. I shake my head. "There isn't anything you can do."

"I'm sorry," he says, "for the way things ended—you know, when I was over at your place."

My heart's doing the *ba-bump* thing so hard I can feel the vibrations in my neck. "Don't worry about it." By which I really mean, *please don't talk about it.* Ollie nods like he gets it. It was just a weird moment. No need to linger on it, right? Except we keep looking at each other, and I have a feeling we're both lingering.

He clenches his jaw and looks away, picking up another book of photography, this time by Dorothea Lange.

I think about what Becca told me. To just tell him what's

really going on. But he's just forgiven me for the way I acted, and if I tell him now, I don't know how he'll react. If he'll tell me he doesn't feel the same way, if he'll remind me that he has a boyfriend, if he'll say he doesn't want to be my friend anymore—same way he ran from me so many years ago.

Ollie and I end up browsing the VHS tapes as we talk about my favorites. I find *Big Fish*, my seventh favorite movie of all time, and I can't hide my shock when he says he hasn't seen it.

"So what's your favorite movie of all time?" he asks.

I know this is supposed to be a hard question, because there're too many good movies to pick just one, but I've always had a favorite, ever since I was a little kid and I watched it with my dad for the first time on the oldies day at the Ridgemont, and I don't hesitate to say it. "*The Princess Bride*." I type on the phone, hand it to him.

Ollie blinks at the phone, blinks at me, then starts to smile—then begins to laugh a little, until he's cracking up so hard he can't even breathe.

"What?" I take the phone away from him. **What's so funny about that?**

He's still laughing. "I don't know," he gasps. "I don't know, I just—I thought you were going to say something serious, like *Memento* or *The Professional* or something like *Amélie*. I just wasn't expecting—"

I can't help but grin. **What do you mean? The Princess Bride**

IS serious—it's one of the best classic films of all time.

He's still laughing, and it's infectious, so the two of us are cracking up in the VHS section.

Ollie and I sit down in the little café area and order iced teas, and we just talk about nothing for a while, stuff that doesn't really matter, and I can't stop grinning, I guess because I'm actually talking to Ollie and acting like a human being again.

Every now and then, Ollie glances at his phone.

"Is it Aiden?" I ask, but he isn't looking at me, so I wave my hand and fingerspell A-I-D-E-N, hooking my finger into a question mark.

He nods. "We're in a fight," he says.

I frown. "About what?"

"He thinks I'm ignoring him. I guess I am, technically. . . . But ever since I moved up here, he's become a little suffocating. He's just texting nonstop, gets angry if I don't respond right away."

I pass him my phone across the table. **Maybe he's scared he's going to lose you.**

Ollie nods, but he doesn't say anything else about that, so I don't either.

When Ollie and I leave, we get on our bus and sit to-gether at the back quietly, a little like the ending scene of *The Graduate*—except our silence is different. It's comfortable. I'm effing ecstatic that it's comfortable. I usually can't go a day without at least one awkward silence, but the quiet that comes over me and Ollie now is the kind where I can tell he's okay with just being together, and I smile to let him know I'm happy with it, too.

It's dark out by the time the bus lets us off near our neighborhood. Ollie walks me back to my place, passing by houses with their windows shining yellow, a car whooshing by. He stops outside my door, the light automatically popping on so that Ollie glows, and I wonder if he expects me to invite him inside. I know my mom would love that, but I hesitate. Things are good now. I don't want to ruin that by getting a hard-on. He'd probably notice it, and things would get weird.

"Today was fun," Ollie says.

I nod my agreement.

"I'm glad we're talking again."

He watches me like he's remembering the last time he was at my house and in my bedroom.

"I, uh—" I start, then pull out my phone. **I'm really sorry for the way I treated you these past few days. For the whole week, I guess.**

He passes the phone back to me. "That's okay."

He's standing there, waiting patiently, probably because he's figured out I have more to say, but I'm having a hard time actually *saying* it, a hard time even breathing. Using the phone makes it easier. **I was really crappy to you because, with the thing** that happened, I guess I kind of liked it, and I freaked out about it.

His lips twitch into a smile, and for a second I have no idea what he's thinking, but then he says, "You liked it?"

My heart's beating hard enough that I'm pretty sure I'm about to pass out. "Yeah."

He lets out a laugh. "I thought you hated me because of it."

"Me, hate you?" I ask. "No—no, I just freaked out because I—I don't know, I guess I was scared, and I—" He's squinting at me, so I stop. Take a breath. Show him my phone. **I was just afraid.**

"I get it." He looks away. "That's what happened to me. You know, before I moved away. I got scared because I liked it and didn't know what that meant. Got scared last week because I liked it when you kissed me, too."

He bites his lip, like maybe he's said too much—watches me. Watches my mouth. I don't know what the hell takes over me. I slide my hand into his. "Is it okay if I kiss you again?"

He opens his mouth and hesitates, pulls his hand from mine. "I'm sorry. I can't do that to Aiden."

Shit. What's worse is that I know they're together—but for that split second, I just didn't care. I nod. "Right. Yeah."

"We said we'd really try long-distance," he tells me. "I don't want to screw it up."

Kind of like how I'm screwing up now. "I'm a jackass."

He shakes his head. "You're not. If it wasn't for Aiden—"

He pauses. "Let's just pretend this didn't happen, okay?"

I nod. "Yeah, that'd be great."

He's still watching me carefully, and I know there's a lot left unsaid, but I can't bring myself to speak. He can't either, apparently.

He clears his throat. "I should go. I'll see you later, okay?"

"All right. Bye."

And—ah, yes, there's the awkward silence. Ollie looks at me a second longer, and I look at him also, and he says bye again, then turns and walks off. And I just stand there, watching him leave. I know my mom is inside, probably on the couch, expecting me to come in any second now since it's almost seven o'clock. But instead of opening the door and going inside, I find myself starting the thirty-minute walk to Flo's. I wasn't really planning it. But my feet are moving, and I know I have to tell her everything.

When I get to Florence's house, the lights in her bedroom window are on, so I know she's home. I don't bother knocking on the door since I know her dad doesn't let her have visitors at night, and since I don't think he likes me very much, for the simple fact that I was dating his daughter. I go for the classic throwing-rocks-at-window scene, and after a few tries, I see a shadow against her lace curtains. She pushes the curtains aside to look down at me, then lets the curtains fall back in place. I stand around for a while, kicking at the stones around my sneakers. Just as I start thinking that she's refusing to come downstairs, the front door opens, and Florence comes out with Tobey Maguire on a leash.

She closes the door and walks along the sidewalk without even looking at me, so I jog over to her to catch up.

"What's on your mind?" she asks me.

"What do you mean?"

"You haven't spoken to me in a while, so I assume something is on your mind."

We walk in quiet for a while.

"You know—this is a weird thing for me to say."

"Just say it, Bird."

"I have a thing for Ollie."

She stops walking, squinting at me. "You have a thing for Ollie? What kind of thing?"

A boner, usually, but I'm not about to say that to her. "I don't know. A thing." I take a breath and turn so that I'm half facing her. "I can't stop thinking about him. I don't know. I really like him."

"Yeah, I do too," she says slowly. "He's a good guy. Really sweet. But that doesn't mean I have a *thing* for him."

I rub my face. I heard once it's supposed to alleviate stress. And it doesn't hurt that it hides my embarrassment. "Whenever I'm near him, I kind of—I don't know, want him. In that way."

"You *want* him?"

"We kind of kissed."

"You *kissed*?"

I don't think that her repeating almost everything I say in that particular tone is a good sign. But I'm confused. She almost seems upset, and I don't really get why. I thought she'd be happy that I'm finally telling her what's been up with me, why I was such an asshole. That she'd see I'm moving on, and she won't have to feel bad that she cheated on me. But instead, she's frowning down at Tobey Maguire.

"I don't really know what to say," she tells me.

"This is awkward."

"I mean, what am I supposed to say? You randomly come over here and tell me you've got a thing for another guy. That you kissed said guy. I mean, I just don't know what to do with that information. What do you expect me to do with it?"

"I don't know."

"Are you looking for my blessing or something?"

That's exactly why I came over, but now I don't think asking her for her permission to have a crush on Oliver James would be the right move. "No, I'm not looking for your blessing," I lie. "I just wanted to tell you why I've been acting weird."

"All right," she says. "Well, thanks."

She turns back for her house without another word, Tobey Maguire scampering on beside her.

"Hey—wait, Flo, what the hell is going on?"

She ignores me. I run up alongside her.

"Are you mad at me or something?"

"Why would I be mad?"

It's clear that she's mad. I just have no idea why. I remember what she said—her fear that she'd turn into my and Ollie's third wheel—but it'd be unfair of her to freak out about that, after the number of times she's made me hang out with her and Lydia. She gets back to her house and lets Tobey Maguire inside, and for a second I think she's planning on slamming the door in my face. But she pauses. She barely looks at me.

"I just need time to process this, all right?" she says.

Then she slams the door in my face.

I can't even move. I'm pretty much shell-shocked. I hold up my hands in a *what the fuck?* way.

I have a thought that's starting to become more and more of a recurring theme in my life: I probably should've just stayed home and watched *Friends* with my mom.

12

IT'S KIND OF INSANE HOW QUICKLY THINGS CAN CHANGE. Days pass and Florence still isn't talking to me, and I don't really know what to say to her, and as someone who is perpetually awkward, when I don't know what to say—well, I just don't speak at all.

Ashley sits with me before school, asking me what happened, saying Flo won't tell her anything. I don't want to admit what Florence and I were talking about before she got pissed. Instead, I lie—say that Flo just got randomly angry. Ash promises me she'll get to the bottom of this with Florence, making me feel even worse for keeping the truth from her.

Things are just as weird with Oliver James—but a different kind of weird. It's been almost a week since I asked if I could kiss him. We haven't spoken about it, even though it's clearly the only thing on our minds. We've been hanging out almost every day now, pretty much nonstop, the way we did when we were kids. We walk to school together in the mornings, hang out in the hallways in between classes, sit together during lunch, laugh and talk and act like it never happened, just like we said we would. Other times, I'll catch him watching me, and I think he might just change his mind about Aiden and lean in to kiss me right there in the middle of school. It's the sort of tension that makes me want to hide from Ollie all over again.

Oliver James and I sit on the damp benches at lunch and finish up our pre-calc homework before class. Ollie's using the calculator on his phone, and I'm trying to pay attention, but failing spectacularly.

"This is making my brain hurt."

Ollie doesn't notice me trying to speak, so I wave at him. He looks up, surprised. I tap my head, point my two index fingers together. I whip out my phone and type up that I really hate pre-calc—hate it with all the burning passion of hell— and he makes the *Y* shape with his hand and points the thumb at himself, nodding.

"Then why're we doing it?"

"Because we'll fail if we don't."

I type on my phone and hand it to him again. **What's the true definition of failing, anyway? I mean, do we really fail just because someone else says so? What if I decide that, by not doing** this homework, I'm actually succeeding at life?

He grins as he hands my phone back. "We fail because we don't graduate."

I slump over, leaning against him heavily, his hair tickling my ear and my neck—making him laugh and try to push me upright again. He's smaller, but he's a pretty strong guy. He's able to hold me up, hands on my shoulders, fingers squeezing lightly, and there's a moment where we both pause, and I feel like the most natural thing would be for him to pull me against him right here in the middle of the courtyard, which wouldn't be the weirdest thing—people hug each other all the time, and I mean, we're friends, so that wouldn't be weird at all.

I see Florence coming over Ollie's shoulder. As soon as I see her, I pull away from him. Flo walks right by, not even looking at us.

"Shouldn't you try talking to her?" Ollie asks.

"You sound like my sister."

He looks like he has something he wants to tell me, but isn't sure how to say it, or doesn't know if he should.

My thumb and pinky pointing out, I tap my knuckles to my chin. "What is it?"

He takes a big breath. "I just feel like I got in between you guys. Like all of this is because of me."

I glance away, flip through the pages of my textbook. "It's not your fault."

I don't think he believes me. And, okay—the smallest part of me, just the slightest sliver of a splinter, doesn't really believe me either. Because, I mean—yeah, shit started hitting the fan when Oliver James got here. But I also know things were already messed up with me and Flo before he came back. It's my problem that I wouldn't let go of what I used to have with Florence. That's not on him.

I hand him my phone. **You didn't do anything.**

He hands back the phone, watching me carefully, before he nods, like he really believes me this time. The bell rings. I wave my hand to let him know, and we walk to his locker. I wait there beside him as he does his combination.

He puts a hand on my arm again, near my elbow, to get my attention. It's just for a second, but I can still feel the heat from his hand there. "Do you want to hang out after school?"

"Sure," I say with a shrug.

"I want to try going somewhere," he says. "To the lake."

"Green Lake?" We used to go there all of the time, but after Ollie left, the place that used to be my favorite reminded me how alone I was, so I haven't been back in years. It's not that far from the school. Maybe half an hour away, if we walk quickly. "Why there?"

"I want to take some photos for my portfolio—you know, for that contest," he says before patting his bag, where I guess he's holding his camera. "I'm kind of hoping you'll be in them." He begins to stuff his books from his locker into his bag.

I wait until he's finished so that he can look at me, hand

outstretched with my phone. **Why do you want me to be in the photos?**

He hesitates, then shrugs. "I don't know. It's just good, I guess, to have subjects to work with, but I don't want to ask a stranger."

There's a pause—the kind of pause that's been happening after I asked if I could kiss him and we haven't talked about it since, and he looks at my mouth. He turns away to zip up his backpack and sling it over his shoulder. "We're going to be late."

"Yeah. Right. Coming."

Green Lake is a little crowded because it's a Friday afternoon, but Ollie and I walk around the trail, water lapping at the edges of the concrete and chilled breeze blowing right through my hoodie and ruffling Ollie's curls. He's got his camera out while he swings his head left and right, until finally he tugs on my arm and points out a shaded and secluded nook, away from the concrete path and onto the dirt, hidden by some trees. The dirt is rocky with smooth stones, and there's a boulder right by the edge of the still water. This was our favorite spot.

I look out at the water that ripples in the breeze, washing up onto the shore of pebbles and gray stones and moss. Ollie turns away and starts fiddling with his camera. I know some stuff about camcorders and white balance and all of that, but what he's doing looks really serious and professional and

151

maybe even a little intimidating.

"You don't mind if I take photos of you, right?" he says, glancing up at me from the camera. "I realized I never actually asked you."

"Oh." I'm not really the kind of guy who likes being in front of cameras a lot, and this could be my chance to get out of it—but something tells me Oliver would be really disappointed, and disappointing him is the last thing I want to do. "I mean. Yeah, it's okay."

He leads me to the boulder and tells me to relax, which is laughable, so I laugh. He's holding the camera beneath him so that his head is turned down while he stares at me through the viewfinder.

"Why's that funny?" he asks.

I don't know how to sign what I'm thinking. "I can't relax."

"Why's that?"

The shutter clicks. I wrap one hand over my stomach, clutching onto my other arm, tapping my temple and shaking my head. "I don't know. I'm just nervous, I guess. Awkward."

He looks up from the viewfinder. "Awkward? Is that what you said?"

I nod.

"Really? You don't seem awkward." He looks back at the camera. His intense focus on the viewfinder—on this image of me—makes it a little hard to concentrate. And breathe.

I point at myself, hold up two thumbs and let one rise

above the other. "I'm the most awkward guy you'll ever meet," I tell him.

"That's not true." The shutter snaps again. "I'm more awkward than you are, for one."

I unfold my arms, shake my upward palms back and forth. "What? No you're not."

"Yeah, I definitely am. I'm still pretty shy, I guess. I never really know what to say to anyone. Or you."

That's surprising. I point my finger at one side of my chest, then the next; tap my palm to the corner of my mouth; turn my finger in a counterclockwise circle. "We talk all the time."

"I know," he says. We stay silent for a minute before Ollie speaks again. "Tell me about films."

I shake my palms back and forth, pinch my fingers together, and let my other hand's index finger rotate in a circle around them, landing on the tips. "What about them?"

The shutter clicks. "Why do you love them so much?"

Christ, what a loaded question. I take a big breath and let my head fall backward and cross my arms before letting the air out through my mouth. Ollie lowers the camera and walks over to me, leans against the boulder beside me, his arm brushing against mine. "A lot of reasons, I guess."

"Like what?"

I hesitate. "I love the way they turn a group of people into one person."

He picks up the camera again—snaps a close-up. "What does that mean?"

I pull my phone out of my pocket, feeling Ollie's eyes on the screen, on my hands, on my face as I type. **When the lights go off in a movie theater, everyone becomes this one entity: the audience watching the film. And most films aim to get the same emotions out of people. The same reactions. To laugh or be scared or cry or be inspired. The audience goes in as individuals and comes out as people who've all experienced the same thing, are all feeling the same way. Well, for the most part.**

Ollie hands back my phone. "I love how excited and passionate you get about movies."

I tap my head, making the Y shape with my hand. "Why's that?"

He holds up the camera again, watching me through the lens. "I feel like I'm seeing a part of you that you don't show very often. It's nice."

I don't say anything to that. I don't really trust myself to speak. I just look at the grass beneath my sneakers.

"I'm sorry. I didn't mean to be weird," he says, lowering the camera.

"That's not weird."

"Oh."

"I wasn't weirded out or anything. Just. I don't know." I tug at the edge of my sleeve. "I wish I could show that side of me a lot more too."

He watches me still, frowning a little—maybe with confusion. Either because he didn't catch what I said, or because he did and he doesn't know what I mean.

"Can we stop?"

He nods. I get up from the boulder. "Sorry, I just—I really hate having my picture taken."

"Really?" Ollie says. "Why didn't you say something?"

"I wanted to make an exception, I guess."

He studies me. "Thank you, Bird. I'm glad you let me take yours."

13

WE WALK BACK TO OUR NEIGHBORHOOD, TOWARD HIS house first. I don't really want to see the photos, but I'm a little surprised he doesn't automatically offer to show them. He must guess what I'm thinking because he says that he still needs to edit them. "Clean up the lighting, that sort of thing. I'll show them to you after, though."

"I don't need to see them. That's okay."

"I want you to see them."

I suck in a big breath. "Okay."

We stop at the top of the hill, outside Oliver James's house. The sun's starting to go down, and the clouds have cleared, so the sky is a dark green. Ollie asks me if I want to come inside. Something tells me that would be an all-around bad idea. We had a good day. I don't need to go inside and inevitably do or say something to fuck it all up. But I nod anyway, and he opens the door, pushing past Donna Noble, who greets us with excited sneezes and a thumping tail. Oliver's mom is sitting in the living room. She gives me a big smile and a hug.

"We're going to be in my room," Ollie says to her over his shoulder.

"Okay," she says, but then reaches out for his shoulder. "Hey," she says, then holds out her fists, thumbs touching each other, puts her palms side by side, swinging one to the side twice, and reaches out a hand as if grabbing onto a doorknob and pulling it to her.

Ollie's ears turn a bright red as he touches one finger to one side of his chest and brings it to the other side, brings a thumb down from his chin while he shakes his head, clamps the fingers of one hand together at his head and brings his hands together, tapping his index fingers together.

Mrs. Hernández smiles and nods. "Sure."

Oliver James shakes his head and walks down the hall, and I follow him into his bedroom. I'm pretty sure I understood the gist of their conversation.

Ollie sits on the edge of his bed, looks up at me. I ask, "Does she make you keep the door open with everyone?"

He rolls his eyes. "It's stupid. She knows I'm going out with Aiden."

I force a laugh. "Yeah."

He lies down on his bed and grabs his laptop. "Want to watch a movie?" he asks without looking at me, so he must already know the answer is yes. I sit beside him, but I don't lie down. I've been making a lot of assumptions about us—but Ollie's right. He's going out with Aiden. We're friends. I have to remember that.

He pulls up *You've Got Mail*—solid choice as far as modern classics go, but yet another romantic comedy.

He turns to look at me, and it strikes me that he was nervous about choosing a movie. "I tried to find a serious film."

I pause, point at him, tap my head, put my index finger on my chin and twist it, hook my finger into a question mark. "You think this is serious?"

He laughs as I cross my legs on the bed, lean back on my hands. "We can watch something else if you want to."

I shake my head. "No, this is fine. It's just—"

He watches me, waiting.

"I don't know." I grab my phone, write up something and toss it over to him. **Romantic comedies piss me off sometimes.**

He glances up at me from the screen. "Somehow that doesn't surprise me."

He turns on the movie and its captions, and we're about halfway through when a notification pops onto the screen for a video chat. Ollie sits up and pauses the movie, glancing at me.

"It's Aiden. I haven't spoken to him all day. Is it okay if I answer?"

Air gets stuck in my throat. "Yeah, of course," I say, then stand off the bed and get out of the way of the web camera. Ollie gives me a grateful smile as I go to the wall with his growing number of photographs—pictures around downtown Seattle, the courtyard at school. I'm trying to give them privacy, but I glance in a mirror propped up against the wall and see Ollie signing. He's got this smile—like yeah, sure, he's smiled at me before—but this smile is the difference between a sun peeking through clouds and blazing on a bright day.

"My friend is here, actually," he says aloud, then waves me over. I hesitate. Wouldn't Aiden be pissed to see me in his boyfriend's bedroom? But Ollie looks at me expectantly and waves me over again, so I move to sit next to Ollie, in front of the camera, so that the two of us are in a box in the corner of the screen.

Aiden looks like he does in his photos—all freckles and straw-colored hair, a big smile. He signs a hello, and I sign a hello back. He points at me, puts a finger from his mouth to his ear and hooks it into a question mark.

I shake my head. "I'm hearing."

He nods. He beckons his hand at his chest, fingerspells O-L-L-I-E, points two hands at his chest, hooks his fingers together. Oliver looks away from the screen.

"Yeah—I mean, I'm glad he's back," I say.

159

Aiden asks me to tell him an embarrassing story about Ollie, and Ollie shakes his head at me, but I laugh and I tell him about that one time in science lab when Oliver James set our teacher on fire, which has Aiden laughing so hard his eyes start to water. Aiden's got this grin, like he's lit up from the inside—the kind of expression people really and truly only make when they're deeply in love, and I know that he loves Ollie. It's easy to see. He turns two fingers over in a circle, motions a *come here* gesture.

Oliver hesitates and glances at me. "I don't know," he says.

"You told your dad you wanted to move back, right?" Aiden says aloud also, his words slurring together slightly.

My heart sinks from my chest and into my stomach. I'm pretty sure that was meant for me to hear. Oliver said his dad was trying to get him to go back to Santa Fe, but Ollie never mentioned he wanted that too. But of course Oliver wants to move back. That's where his life has been for the past five years. It's where his boyfriend is, his friends. It's stupid of me to assume that he's happy here, just because we're hanging out again.

Ollie looks at me. "Dad wants me to come back, but . . ." He puts a hand to his temple, turns it away while shaking his head. He puts a flat palm to his face, thumb tapping his chin, and holds up one finger, turning it in a circle.

Aiden points at his chin and points at Ollie. Oliver James sighs, turns to me.

"Can you give us a minute, Bird?"

I nod. "Yeah, of course. You know, actually, it's getting kind of late. I should probably just go home."

Ollie frowns. "Are you sure? We haven't finished the movie."

"We can finish it another time." I tell Aiden it was nice to meet him, and he smiles as he signs goodbye. Ollie gets up to walk me out his door, into the living room where Donna Noble is curled up at his mom's feet.

"It was nice hanging out," he says. "Thanks for letting me take your photos."

I nod. "No problem."

He looks like he wants to say something else, but he just takes a big breath and opens the door for me, not speaking or signing as I tell Mrs. Hernández goodnight and walk outside.

The sun moves fast and the sky has streaks of red and orange by the time I make my way down the hill. As I get closer, I can see that Florence is waiting for me on the front steps of my house. I slow down to a stop in front of her. She does a one-handed wave.

"Hi, Nate."

"Hi, Flo."

"Can we talk for a second?"

I nod, and I sit down beside her. Her chin is on top of her knees, swaying back and forth.

"I'm not really sure what to say," she tells me.

"Yeah, I know," I say, a little embarrassed that my voice comes out a little too deep, a little too emotional. "I'm not sure what to say either."

"This is stupid." She finally looks up at me. "What the hell happened to us?"

It has to be a rhetorical question, because she has a much better idea of what the hell happened, since I still have no fucking clue. I don't say anything to that.

"I'm sorry," she says. "This whole thing is stupid."

"Then why wouldn't you speak to me?"

"It's like I was watching myself. I knew I was being ridiculous, but I couldn't stop because I was so pissed off. You really pissed me off."

Hearing that actually kind of pisses me off. "What the hell did I do, Flo?"

She sighs. "I should've told you this weeks ago. Lydia's been wanting to break up with me. I kept convincing her not to, but that night you came over—she decided to end things."

"What?"

"But that isn't even the point."

"No, wait—what?"

"Seriously, Bird, let me finish." She pauses, as if really making sure that I don't have any plans to interrupt her again, before she goes on. "Lydia broke up with me, and I'm still sad and frustrated because of that, and then it felt like I was losing you too. I mean, you said you have a thing for Ollie, when you used to have a thing for me. And you told me I wouldn't be your third wheel, even though that's clearly what I'm becoming."

"You *aren't* becoming—"

"Just let me finish. I thought I'd lost you, and I wasn't sure what to do to stop it. I wasn't sure if I even could stop it."

I watch her.

"I'm finished now. Your turn to say something."

"There wasn't anything to stop. You weren't losing me."

Her knees have stopped swaying back and forth, but she's picking at something on the step, not looking at me. "Have I lost you now?"

"No," I tell her. I don't know that's the answer until it comes out, but then I realize it's true. "No, you haven't."

She smiles into her knees and nudges me with her shoulder. "Thanks."

We're both quiet, but not in an awkward silence. I can tell that we're both just thinking, taking a second to process the past minute of conversation. This is a lot to process.

"Lydia broke up with you?"

She nods. "It's a long story."

"I'd never choose Ollie over you, you know. There's nothing to choose. You already know how I feel about you. I'm not going to stop being friends with you, just because I'm friends with Ollie, or because I have a thing for him."

"You're right." She shakes her head. "None of that was fair of me to say."

We sit together on the edge of the steps. It begins to drizzle a little, but neither of us moves. She rests her head on the side of my shoulder.

"What happened with Lydia?" I ask her.

"What usually happens," she says. "Two humans realized they're not right for each other."

I put my arm over her shoulder. A few weeks ago, I would've thought twice about it. Would've worried she'd realize I'm still in love with her. But now, I put my arm over her shoulder because she's my friend. And I think that's okay.

"I really miss her," she says. "She's an amazing illustrator. Did I ever show you any of her art?"

"No, you never showed me."

"Well, fuck that shit," she says. "I'm not going to show you now." She laughs and wipes her eyes. She tells me that Lydia had wanted an open relationship—felt suffocated by Florence. "She wanted to break up with me, but I convinced her not to—but finally she texted me saying it's over. She started dating some surfer," Flo says, rolling her eyes.

"I'm sorry, Flo."

"I'm kind of embarrassed by myself," she says. "I would've told anyone else to get the fuck over it instead of begging to stay in a relationship, even though I wasn't wanted."

"Don't be so hard on yourself."

She smiles a little. "I tell the same thing to you all the time." She smiles at me. "I've really missed you."

"I've missed you, too."

"I'd started to realize that the way I was acting was bullshit, but I felt like the fight was too far along to really stop it."

"It wasn't really a *fight*, was it?"

She gives me a look. "I'm pretty sure it was a fight."

"A disagreement, maybe."

"We were fighting, Nate."

She leans back against the stairs, stretching her legs out. "You've got a thing for Ollie," she says, a little slowly. It's almost like we're continuing that conversation from a few nights ago.

"Yeah," I say hesitantly.

"What does that mean?" she says. "Are you—in love with him?"

Good question. I want him in *that* way, and I can't stop thinking about him—but does that mean I'm in love with him? Do I love him the same way that I love Florence? Maybe the way you love changes from person to person.

I shake my head. "I don't know. I'm still trying to figure that part out."

She nods. "Okay. No pressure to figure anything out, you know?"

"Yeah."

She takes my good arm and kisses my cheek. "You're such a great guy," she says. "Ollie's really lucky you have a thing for him."

I laugh. "I don't know if I'd say that. I mean—everything's

been so messy. I haven't even seen Oliver James in years." And now he's going to move back to Santa Fe to be with his boyfriend.

"It isn't weird. It's cute."

"Cute?"

"Yes. Cute. And human. All of this confusing shit between you? That's what humans do. And, what, is there a required time limit for how long you're supposed to know someone, before you're allowed to feel something for them? That's ridiculous."

God, I've missed her. "I don't know. There's no point anyway. He wants to move back to Santa Fe."

"What? When?"

"I don't know. He and his boyfriend started to video chat, and that's what Aiden said. Ollie's talked about moving back before, but he said he wanted to stay here because of his mom."

"So he's not officially leaving yet?" She knocks a hand into my knee. "Bird, you have to say something."

"What?"

"Tell him how you feel. You never know—maybe he feels the same way, and he'll want to stay."

I think about the day Ollie moved back to New Mexico and I kissed him. He ran away then, stopped speaking to me altogether. What's to say he wouldn't do the same if I tell him how I feel now? "I don't know. I don't think that's a good idea."

Her smile instantly vanishes. "Why not?"

There's a split second of silence before the sky opens up and rain pours down. I'm instantly soaked through. We jump up from the steps, and I try opening the door, but it's locked. I check my pockets, but my keys aren't there. "Shit."

"Where's your mom?" Flo shouts over the sheets of rain smacking the pavement.

"On a date, I think. She's trying to get out there again."

"Oh. That's inconveniently sweet."

I look around, then pull her hand and run until we're under the edge of the roof of the garage. We stand there, shivering and watching the rain. It's quieter under here, so I don't have to shout anymore. "I don't know if I should tell him. I'm just kind of happy we can even be friends. I don't want to ruin anything."

She smiles at me. "Nate. You're ruining what could be a really amazing relationship by *not* telling him."

I can't help but grin. I shake my head. "I hate it when you say smart shit."

She looks away, fingers twirling one of her twists. "I really loved when we were together, you know."

I clench my jaw and look away from her. "Why'd you break up with me, then?"

It's a conversation we've had a million times, but maybe it's a conversation we need to keep having, until we're both used to the idea that we're not together anymore. "I'd kissed

Lydia. I couldn't be with you after that."

"I forgave you. I was willing to keep trying."

"But I knew I couldn't keep trying when I had feelings for someone else—and when I just didn't feel the same way about you anymore."

It still hurts to hear, even after all this time.

"I know we're better for each other as friends," she says. "I don't want to lose that. We're really great friends, Nate."

"Yeah. I know."

My mother's car swings into the driveway. The garage door begins to open behind us, and we step out of the way. The car drives by and parks in its spot, and my mom steps out of the car, surprised.

"Did you get locked out?" she asks.

I try not to look too ashamed. "Maybe."

She lets us inside, seems genuinely happy to see Florence even though she knows what happened between us now, and I drag Flo away from the living room before we can be trapped there. My mom reminds us of the open-door policy, which is really embarrassing, but Flo just laughs and settles onto my bed as I grab my laptop.

"I'm thinking a ridiculously bad sequel," I say, sitting down next to her and getting to Netflix. "*Mean Girls 2? Bring It On 4?*"

"*Mean Girls 2*, definitely."

I type it in, click on the link. We sit together, watch as the fanfare begins. Something catches Florence's eye—she looks at my desk, then reaches for my spiral-bound notebook, open and resting on top of Robert McKee's *Story*. It's supposed to be filled with notes from biology, but it mostly has really bad ideas for my script. I lean forward to snatch it away, but she keeps the notebook out of reach, still staring at the page of ideas as she holds it above her head.

"What's this?" she asks, then pulls the book out of reach again when I lunge.

"Nothing—just notes for my script. Give it back!"

She stands up, head quirked in curiosity as she reads. "Dinosaurs return to earth? A woman goes on a mission for revenge?"

I get to my feet, grab the notebook back from her, ignore that she looks like she's trying very hard not to laugh.

I toss it back onto my desk. "Okay, all right. I know they're not the most original ideas."

"You know," she says as she sits back on the edge of my bed, "the best stories draw from real life."

"So I've been told." I shrug. "I guess I don't have much to write about."

She fake-gasps. "Seriously? I'm not inspiring enough?"

I roll my eyes and jump back onto the bed. The first scene starts.

"What about Ollie?" she asks.

I glance at her. "What do you mean?"

"Maybe you should write about him. Since, you know, you're so in love with him and everything." She nudges me with her shoulder.

"I'm not exactly a rom-com kind of guy."

"Who said it has to be a rom-com?" she says. "Just—you know. Write about how you feel."

We go back to watching the movie—but suddenly, my thoughts are spiraling. A script, inspired by Oliver James.

I reach for my notebook again, grab a pen, and start scribbling. I can feel Florence smiling as she watches the movie.

14

I THINK ABOUT WHAT FLORENCE SAID OVER AND OVER again nonstop: tell Ollie how I feel. Maybe she's right. Maybe he'll feel the same way.

Oliver James walks with me to school in the morning, hangs out with me between classes and during lunch. I feel awkward around him now—struggle to find neutral topics of conversation. My writing, Ollie's photography, the Emerging Creatives contest. I just have two months now. There's literally no way in hell that I can write a script in two months. But Oliver James talks about it with so much excitement that it's hard to tell him I don't think I can apply after all.

"It'd be great to go to New York together," he says. "We could be roommates. And who knows—maybe we'd love it so much that we could go back for college after we graduate, right?"

I can't do anything but nod, my heart beating just a little harder. When we head off in different directions for class, I give an awkward wave and duck my head as I make my escape.

I get to statistics and automatically start walking to the back to join Gideon and Ashley—but they're facing each other, and Gideon's face is red—his eyes wet. Ashley's holding his hand. I slow down, and Ash looks up, sees me—

"Oh, Bird," she says, dropping Gideon's hand.

Gideon doesn't even look at me. He just leans back in his seat and stares forward at the front of the class, rubbing his nose.

"Hey," I say, sliding into my seat, staring at Gideon. "Everything all right?"

"Oh, yeah, everything's fine," Ashley says, flipping open her notebook. "Did you hear there's a pop quiz?"

I'm having a hard time looking away from Gideon—I've never seen him this worked up before—but he's not meeting my eyes, and Ash was more than obvious with the subject change. I feel a twinge of hurt that Gideon's not trusting me with whatever's going on . . . but it's not like I'm the prime example of what *sharing feelings* looks like.

"No, I didn't know," I tell Ashley.

"Here, let's study before the bell rings," she says, grabbing her textbook, glancing at Gideon one more time.

At the end of the day, I get home and open the front door, kick off my sneakers, and walk to the kitchen, dropping my backpack on the floor. My mom's sitting at the counter.

"Hey, Mom." I head for the fridge, but pause when she doesn't answer. When I glance at her over my shoulder, she's leaning against the white granite, arms crossed. A pile of papers are beside her. My application for the Emerging Creatives contest.

She gives me a look that lets me know it's time to get the hell out of there. I pretend I didn't notice the application, slam the fridge door shut so hard that everything inside rattles, and make it halfway down the hall before she says my name.

I take a deep breath as I turn around and stand in the kitchen entrance.

She holds up a piece of paper with an unreadable expression. "What is this?"

I know exactly what it is. I printed out the application because I'm an old man and didn't feel like staring at it on my laptop screen. I'd put it under a stack of books on my desk, so my mom must've gone through my things. Like I'm some untrustworthy teenager.

"What is this?" she asks again, more slowly this time.

I decide to play dumb. "What is what?"

She slaps the paper to the kitchen counter. "Did you apply to this?"

I don't answer.

"*Nathan Bird*, you know better than to ignore me when I ask you a question."

I close my eyes and take a deep breath. "The Emerging Creatives contest. It's for high schoolers who want to go to college for a creative field. If I win, I get a summer of free screenwriting classes."

My mom doesn't even pause. "Where would you take the classes?"

I rub the back of my neck. "At a university," I say. She waits. "In New York."

"Oh, Nate." She sighs, turns away.

"Becca is in Chicago."

"Rebecca is in college. *You're* not."

"I have to go to college someday too. This could be—I don't know, a stepping-stone. Practice."

"You didn't ask me if you could apply to something like this."

"I didn't think I'd need your permission."

"To fly across the country? Of course you would need my permission, Nate."

"I'm going to end up flying across the country eventually anyway."

She doesn't say anything to that, and I think I might've hurt her feelings, because she really might've hoped I'd stay here in Seattle—but a part of me is angry enough not to care.

She didn't have a right to go through my things. She doesn't have a right to tell me what I can and can't do for the rest of my life. She can't tell me *not* to apply to this.

"I don't need your permission to apply."

"You're sixteen."

"Exactly. I'm not a little kid anymore."

She shakes her head. "I think you need to spend your summer more constructively."

"It is constructive, if screenwriting is what I want to do for the rest of my life."

"You don't know if this is really what you want to do yet."

"I'm pretty sure I know what I want more than you."

She gives me a warning look. "I don't think I'm comfortable with the idea of you leaving for an entire summer to stay across the country by yourself. Discussion over," she says when I open my mouth to argue.

"No," I say. "Discussion not over—"

"I don't want to hear about this again." She waves one of the papers in the air. "Okay?"

I clench my jaw and leave the kitchen. Fume and pace around my room. Sit down on the edge of my bed and open my laptop and force myself to start writing, because I already know I have to apply. No matter what my mom thinks.

Ollie waits for me on the corner the next morning so that we can take the walk to school together. One look at me and he grimaces. He points at me, uses his right palm to cut against his left, hooks his finger into a question mark. "Rough night?"

"Is it that obvious?"

He actually looks concerned. "You just look tired. What happened?"

I shrug, try to make it seem like it's not such a big deal. "I just pulled an all-nighter."

He stops walking, mouth falling open. "An all-nighter?" he says. "Did you say all-nighter?"

My first thought is that it's a cute expression. My second thought is that I'm losing my damn mind. "Kind of, yeah."

"What'd you do that for? Did we have a test I forgot about?"

"No," I say quickly. I pull out my phone, hand it to him. **No test. And I guess all-nighter is an exaggeration. I went to bed at four.**

"But . . . why?"

I take a deep breath. "I was trying to get my script finished for the Emerging Creatives contest." I type up a quick explanation. **My mom told me I can't apply, and I spent the whole night trying to write because she pissed me off.** He looks up, raising an eyebrow at me, and I tell him, "I guess I don't even know if it was worth it."

"What do you mean?"

There's no way I'm going to win.

"Why not?"

I shrug and try to make it seem like I don't care. **I kind of suck at writing. A lot.**

Now he has this incredulous look on his face. "Why do you think that?"

"I mean. I don't know." **Talent's pretty easy to see. Like you. You're really talented at photography.**

His ears start to turn a little red, and he tugs on one of them as he hands my phone back to me. "Thanks."

I start typing on my phone, and I can't stop. All of my fears, all of my insecurities, end up in the notes section. After all the typing, I shake my head—think about deleting all of it, just putting the phone back in my pocket, but Ollie reaches out his hand with his brows knitted, and I put it in his palm.

My writing is nowhere near as good as your photography. It's not as serious. It's empty. I start questioning the point of my writing all over again. If I'm not adding anything important to the world, then why am I writing? The deadline is in two months, and I'm still nowhere near finished. Even my all-nighter only got me ten pages, after all of the deleting and rewriting. The script is a mess. If I don't win the contest or even get one of the ten spots, what does that mean? That I'm not meant to be a screenwriter?

Ollie scrolls, reading—seems engrossed reading what's practically a novel on my phone. He looks up at me, hands the phone back, seems to think for a second. "Well, none of us think we're really any good at anything. Most times, turns out we're not."

My eyebrows raise. Most times, people just say something

177

like, "I'm sure you're great."

He pauses, then continues, "You could be shit at it. That doesn't mean you should stop."

He claps his hands together for a second, thinking carefully about his words, before he keeps speaking. "If you feel the need to do it—to write, or paint, or take photos, or anything—then that's what you have to do. That's the one most important thing that you can do. Because if you don't, then there isn't any point to anything, right? You've got to do it. You've got to keep writing."

He looks so serious, so determined to make me understand, that I can't help but laugh a little. That doesn't faze him. "I'm serious, Bird."

"I know."

We walk silently for a while before he tells me, "I want to read your script."

I shake my head quickly. "Oh, I don't know—"

"Someone has to read it sometime." He tells me something else, but the sounds blur together, and I'm not sure what he said, but he continues. "If someone's waiting to read it, maybe that'll help you hit your deadline."

I already know that showing him this script would be an all-around bad idea. I'm writing it because of him—practically for him—but I don't want him to read it. Don't want him to know how much I think about him. Besides—he might find it creepy if he realizes he's the inspiration.

I swallow. "Yeah. Maybe."

He's biting his bottom lip now, watching me. "You're not going to send me the script, are you?"

I shake my head. "To be honest? Probably not."

He nods. "Okay. At least you told me the truth."

We turn a corner, start walking through the middle of a park, passing by the playground, toddlers screaming and laughing as adults watch on the bench.

"Ollie," I say, "are you really going back to Santa Fe?"

He doesn't see me—he's looking at the kids with a faint smile on his face. I think about just letting it go, not asking again, but I have to know. I tap his shoulder so that he'll look at me. I use both my fingers, pointing forward, and fingerspell S-A-N-T-A F-E, hooking a finger into a question mark.

He pauses as he begins to crack his knuckles. "I wish Aiden hadn't said anything."

"So you do want to go back?"

He shrugs. "I miss Aiden. My dad. My friends."

I nod. "Yeah, I get it."

"But I'd also miss my mom if I left," he says. "I don't want to leave her alone." He glances at me. "And you. I'd also miss you."

My heart starts beating a little too fast. "Really?" I say. "I mean, I'd miss you, too."

We walk without speaking or signing for a while. Turn another corner, and we pass the soccer field that Gideon's team sometimes uses for practice and matches.

Ollie says, "I'm thinking of breaking up with Aiden."

I stop walking. Ollie doesn't notice for a few steps, until he stops and glances back at me, this worried look on his face. I tap my temple, bring my fingers into the Y shape.

"The long-distance thing," he says, hesitating, before he adds, "it's not working out. Aiden's frustrated and really wants me to move back, and I don't like feeling the pressure to move back just for him. Plus he was weirdly jealous when he saw us together—thinks I'm going to cheat on him—"

I bite my lip. Because of me—because I kissed him—he technically has.

Ollie's watching me. "I don't know. I'm only thinking about it at this point. Let's keep walking."

We keep walking. I swallow, looking at him out of the corner of my eye, but he only stares forward as we come toward the school, lost in thought.

I wave for his attention, rub a fist around my chest in a circle.

He frowns at me. "Why?"

"I don't know. You and Aiden just seemed really happy."

"We were," he says. "It's no one's fault that I moved away."

But I can't help but think about what Aiden must be going through. I guess because I know how it feels to lose Oliver James.

* * *

The possibility of Ollie breaking up with Aiden follows me like a cloud, putting my head into a fog. I catch myself day-dreaming in the middle of biology, literally staring at the back of Ollie's head, wondering what it might be like—the possibility of a single Oliver James. The possibility of asking him out, of him saying yes.

The cloud follows me all the way to the greenhouse when the lunch bell rings, and my heart starts hammering at the idea of sitting with him and talking to him and acting like everything's the same as always, but when I open the door, only Florence and Ashley are there. I try to pretend I'm not disappointed.

I plop onto the bench beside Ash. "Where's Ollie and Gideon?"

"You'd know where Oliver James is better than us," Florence says, sketching in a notebook.

"Oh, I think he's actually doing something for his photography class," Ashley says, not looking up from her textbook.

"And Gideon?"

She takes a second to answer, shifting on the bench, still staring at the page in front of her. "I don't know. Maybe an emergency student council meeting?"

I frown, leaning back against the tabletop, the corner digging into my back. "Is everything okay with him?"

She glances up with wide eyes. "Yeah. Why wouldn't it be?"

"Because he was crying in statistics."

Florence looks up with a frown. "Gideon was crying? Why?"

Ashley purses her mouth. "Gideon's allowed to cry, you know."

"We know," Florence says. "That's not the issue. The issue is *why*. Is he all right?"

Ashley closes her textbook. "I don't feel comfortable saying anything without Gideon's permission. He's going through something—but that's all I'll tell you. When he's ready, he'll say what's going on. Okay?"

I glance at Florence. This is maybe the first time I've seen Ashley ever keep a secret. It must be pretty serious. "Yeah—okay," I say.

She nods, reassured, and starts to pack her bag. "I'm going to keep studying in the AP English classroom."

Florence and I don't say anything as she leaves.

"What the hell?" Flo whispers.

"I don't know. I'm actually kind of freaking out."

"Me too," she says, grabbing a carrot stick and biting half with a snap.

We sit in silence for a while, and I consider telling her about Oliver James and Aiden—that Oliver is considering breaking up with him—but I know if I tell her, she'll just demand I tell Ollie how I feel immediately. Besides, it isn't my business to tell.

Flo glances at me. "You okay?"

I nod. "Yeah. I'm fine."

We go back to sitting in silence.

15

I'M LATER THAN USUAL TO SCHOOL THE NEXT MORNING. I pulled another almost all-nighter, forcing myself to write, to try to finish at least this script. It's all complete shit, but at least I'm writing—and with the deadline speeding toward me, I have to keep going.

Florence sits at our regular bench in the courtyard with Ashley and Gideon. Ash and Gideon sit off to the side, speaking in low voices—about whatever secret Gideon doesn't want us knowing, I guess. Florence sketches in the margins of her notebook. I plop down beside her, resting my head in my arms. It's like the tension of the past few days—Oliver James, the bullshit with this script, the lack of sleep . . .

"Are you okay?" Florence asks.

And the thing is, I don't know if I am. I think I'm a pretty stable guy. Down-to-earth, reasonable, always trying to do the good thing—the usual defining attributes of any average sixteen-year-old junior. But now—suddenly I feel like I'm on the edge of a meltdown.

Florence crosses her arms. "You really should just talk to him," she says to me.

I give her a look. Amazed that she would even bring it up. She shrinks back a little and shrugs, mouthing, "What?" Like it's no big deal she'd mention my deepest, darkest secret right here, right now, in front of Ashley and Gideon.

Gideon glances over at me, feigning innocent curiosity. "Him who?"

"No one," I say a little too quickly.

Ashley and Gideon are looking at each other now.

"Well, *that* isn't suspicious at all," Gideon says. "It's not like you speak to a lot of people. So if it's a guy, it's probably either me or Oliver. You have something you need to say to me, Bird?"

"Jesus, would you just drop it?" Florence says. Trying to backtrack and make up for her mistake. Too little, too late, Flo.

"You're the one that brought it up."

"Yeah. And now I'm bringing it back down."

Gideon ignores her and squints at me. "You would've just told me if you had something on your mind. So you've got something to tell Oliver James."

Ashley is watching me very carefully. A little too carefully.

I decide the best way to get out of this is to literally, physically leave the bench. I'm grabbing my bag and muttering some excuse about class when Ashley gasps and claps her hand over her mouth.

"*That's* why he wasn't interested in me," she says.

I look at Flo. Her face mirrors mine: pure horror. "What?"

"When you spoke to Ollie for me—you said he wasn't interested. It's because you two already have a secret love affair."

I slump back to the bench. "No. No."

"Ashley, listen to me," Florence says. "That is so not the case."

Gideon's nodding, still squinting his eyes at me. "Yeah. That makes sense," he says.

"What? No it doesn't," I say.

He keeps going. "You two are always together. I mean, sitting together, talking and shit—"

"Because we're *friends*."

"Bullshit. There's definitely something else going on."

"Jesus Christ."

Florence takes in this sharp breath that just grabs everyone's attention, and she raises both hands like she's about to swear to tell the whole truth and nothing but the truth, and then she slaps her knees and says, "We should just tell them."

I could actually kill her. She's giving me this apologetic look. But I mean, it's fucked up, right? It wasn't her decision to make. She shouldn't have even brought it up in the first place.

Gideon smirks. "So it's true. I mean, it's pretty obvious. You said he was hot that first day."

"Oh my fucking God. I only said that to shut you up."

"You could've said he was ugly. Would've worked like a charm."

Florence just keeps shaking her head. Ashley is watching me, clearly trying not to smile because apparently she thinks this is all so romantic, and Gideon is just sitting there with his smug-ass smile.

"Okay," I say. "All right."

Gideon smirks. "Called it."

"We're not *together*," I say, mostly in Ash's direction. Her smile falls a little. "I just—I don't know, have a thing for him. It's a small thing. Not a big deal at all."

"I'd say it's a pretty big deal," Gideon says.

"I might actually agree with that," Ashley adds.

"Christ. It's not a big deal." I rake my hands through my hair, seconds away from yanking a couple of strands right out of my head. "We're not going out or anything."

"But you want to go out with him, right?" Ashley asks.

There's no point in lying at this point. "Yeah, but he has a boyfriend."

Ashley crosses her arms. "Have you at least told him how you feel?"

"No."

"Oh," Gideon says. "You should definitely tell him how you feel."

Flo raises her hands into the air with an *I told you so* expression. Funny how easily she betrays me without a second thought.

"Why is everyone saying that?"

"Because it's true," Florence says. "I mean, if even Gideon thinks so—"

"That's offensive."

"Then, I mean, it has to be true. You'd make a pretty cute couple."

Shit. I legitimately don't know if I can take this anymore. I'm not the kind of guy who really does well with my business, my personal life, my feelings out on display. But Ashley is smiling at me from across the table. She reaches out and takes my hand and squeezes it.

"I really hope that it works out," Ashley says. "That you become boyfriend and boyfriend, and you become high school sweethearts, and you get married and have really beautiful children."

"Uh. Thanks, Ash."

She pats my hand.

The bell rings, and I haven't seen Ollie this morning yet, which actually kind of worries me. He wasn't at the corner when I left, so I assumed he'd gotten here before me—but with Gideon and Ash now pretty much watching my every move,

I feel like I can't say anything about it. I'm dreading the next time all five of us are sitting together and hanging out. They're probably going to do nothing but stare at us. I get my bag and head toward the front doors with Florence, listening to her apologize on repeat.

Ollie comes across the courtyard. Just the sight of him makes it a little harder to breathe. I can already feel Gideon's and Ashley's stares burning into me. Oliver waves and signs to me that he slept through his alarm clock before hurrying inside—his first class is on the other side of campus—but his cheeks are red and his eyes are glassy, like he's been crying. I text him as I walk into my first class with Flo.

Hey, are you okay?

My phone buzzes a second later.

Yeah. I just had a fight with Aiden.

About what?

He told me that he's tired of the long-distance thing, and said that if I don't move back to New Mexico he's going to break up with me.

My fingers hesitate over the screen. **Do you think he will?**

I told him I couldn't move back just for him. He got mad.

I shouldn't be this happy, this relieved, that they're having issues. **Maybe you can visit Santa Fe.** That's what I text him, but I instantly regret it. What if he goes and decides not to come back?

I get another text after a minute. **I think I might.**

He doesn't say anything else for a while, until another text appears. He has something to show me, and is it okay if he drops by my house after school? He can't walk back with me because of a project for his photography class, but he can meet me later.

Yeah, sure, that's okay.

I'm lying in bed, watching *Forrest Gump*, which is—you know—just all kinds of a freaking amazing movie. It's my eleventh favorite film of all time. Watching makes me hate myself a little, because I know I'll never be that good. Showing so much life and love, all packed into two and a half hours, in a way that makes me fall a little more in love with life and the world and myself—that's incredible.

I get a text from Ollie saying he's on his way. Ever since he said he had something to show me, I've been trying to rack my brain to figure out what it could be. This'll be the first time he's been over since the night I kissed him. I try not to think about that too much.

I go downstairs and stop by the door. Which might be a little weird, I guess, just standing there like a dog waiting for his human to come home. He knocks, and I wait a few seconds before I reach for the doorknob. It's like opening the door to a flood of sunshine.

He asks, "Can I come in?"

"Shit. Yeah. Of course."

He steps inside, and I lead the way to my room. He walks in, kicks off his sneakers, and immediately goes straight to the shelves where I have my old VHS tapes and DVDs and books. "These are—" He says a word, I'm not sure which; could be *incredible*. "Did you get a lot of these at that store? Sparrow and Nightingale?"

I nod and sit on the edge of my bed. Hope he doesn't plan on looking at my lap any time soon.

He slides his bag off his shoulder and walks over, setting it down at my feet. He kneels down and rummages through until he finds a folder. He pulls it out and hands it to me, then sits down next to me. Sitting close enough that our arms accidentally brush up against each other.

I hesitate. "What is it?"

"Open it."

I do. Inside are the photos he took at the lake. Photos of me. It's immediately embarrassing, and I don't want to look—especially not when he's there watching me, waiting for a reaction—but I don't want to just dismiss them—to dismiss him. I take a breath and pull them out of the folder.

Three photos, each in black and white. One has me standing at the very edge of the frame, cut off a little, facing the water and the sky, which looks never-ending. Then the other is a little closer: me, right in the middle of the frame, my hand clutching my other arm, looking extremely nervous and uncomfortable. The last one is a wide shot of my face—my shoulders, my neck, my head, and the trees behind me taking up most of the frame. The branches look like they're sprouting right out of my hair.

"That one's my favorite," he says.

I think it's mine too.

"It looks like you don't belong in this world."

"Do I look that ridiculous?"

He shakes his head. "No, I mean, it looks like you're too good for this world. I don't know. That's just the feeling I get when I see it."

I look at him, and he's already looking at me, waiting like he'd be happy to just sit there and watch me, and I get this overwhelming feeling to kiss him—but I force myself to break the stare and turn to the photos again.

I point at the pictures, extend a finger from my mouth, put an open palm on top of my other palm. "These are really good, Ollie."

"Thanks, Bird."

"Really, really good." I pull out my phone, type in the notes. **You're going to end up famous or something.**

"I wouldn't go that far." He hesitates. "I really liked taking your photos."

I'm not sure what to say. What's an appropriate response to that? I put the tips of my fingers against my mouth, extend my palm toward him.

"I'd really like to take your photo again. Not right now,"

he adds, "but sometime. Would that be okay?"

I nod. "Yeah. That'd be okay."

We end up watching *Forrest Gump* together. I put on the captions. Ollie makes himself more comfortable, lying down on his stomach, so I can see the way his shoulder blades poke out from his shirt and curve down to a strip of boxer shorts peeking out from his jeans. We're well into the film when I'm not sure if I can take that curve in his back anymore. Forrest begins his three-year run, and the screen shows those beautiful mountains and lakes and never-ending roads, and all I can do is stare at Oliver James's back.

I glance up. Ollie's watching me stare at him. "You okay?"

I reach for my phone, hand it to him. **I hope I didn't mess up things between us. You know, that day you came over, and you were upset.**

"No. No, you didn't mess anything up."

"I keep making mistakes."

"Mistakes?"

I nod. "Yeah." **Keep hoping you feel the same way that I do.**

He frowns, squinting at me, like he wants to make sure he doesn't miss anything I'm saying. "How do you feel?"

I hesitate. **I've kind of had feelings for you since we were kids.** I type, looking away as I hand it back to him. **I still do.**

Oliver doesn't speak, doesn't move. It takes everything for me to stay where I am—to not run away.

He says, "I broke up with Aiden."

"What?" I look at him to see if he's joking, but his blank expression seems serious enough. "When?"

"Right before I came over."

"What made you—"

Ollie leans forward and kisses me, pulls back just enough for me to feel his breath on my lips—I grab him, pull him against me, our mouths pressed together, and we fall sideways, his hands in my hair and on my shoulders and under my shirt, one leg in between mine so I know he can feel *exactly what the hell is going on there* while my mouth trails away from his and to his neck, my hands wrapped around his back to press him as close to me as possible—

He gasps, sits up and pulls away from me. "Shit. I'm sorry. I didn't mean to—"

"No, no—it's okay, really," I say, breathing hard, still staring at his lips, leaning forward again—but he puts a hand out against my chest. He has to feel how hard and fast my heart is beating.

"No, it's not," he says. "I just broke up with Aiden. And you—it's so up and down with you—back and forth, I never know what you're thinking or feeling. One second you're ignoring me, the next we're back to being friends."

Christ. To go from hot, seriously effing hot making out, to a sobering conversation like this—I close my eyes, breathe. "I didn't mean to ignore you. I was just afraid."

"I don't know what you're saying."

I smooth a hand over my face, search the sheets for my

phone—find it on the floor, one of us must've knocked it over—and type quickly, hand it to him.

He looks up at me. "Afraid of what?"

Everything I was starting to feel, I guess. I knew you didn't feel the same way.

He frowns. "You can't decide how I do and don't feel. How do you know I haven't felt the same way?"

Because you literally ran away from me when we were kids.

He shrugs. "We were kids. I was scared."

"And now?"

He clenches his jaw, looks away. "I don't know. It's like I'm caught in between Seattle and Santa Fe." I hadn't even considered that. Just because he broke up with Aiden doesn't mean he'll stay here in Seattle. "You're not the deciding factor, but you're a part of it—but I don't know how you feel about me. Sometimes it's like you hate me."

I rub my hands over my face. "I like you," I admit. Maybe even love, but I can't bring myself to say it aloud, not yet. "And I want to be with you."

"But?"

"But, I—I don't know." I start typing. **I'm surrounded by these relationships that always crash and burn.**

"What relationships?"

"Me and Florence, Florence and Lydia, your parents—"

He's shaking his head. "What does that have to do with us?"

I just keep typing. **And then there's my dad, and I see what his** death did to my mom. I don't know. You never know what'll happen. He's confused, so I say, "If one of us gets hurt, or . . ." I don't want to lose you again.

Realization dawns on Ollie's face. "But it's not fair of you to decide all of that on your own. It's like you've already doomed our relationship before even giving it a chance."

But our relationship already *is* doomed—I want to explain it to him, but I can't find the right words.

"And besides," he says. "Even if it doesn't work out, that doesn't mean you'll lose me. You're still friends with Florence, right?"

I have no choice but to nod.

"I don't want to lose you again either," he says. He raises his hands, and I think he's going to sign, but then he just takes my hands and squeezes them. "And the best way to make sure that doesn't happen is to be together, right?"

The fear inside is still bubbling up, but I can't tell him no—not again, not when I want him as much as I do. I nod, and he smiles before leaning forward. He kisses one corner of my mouth, the way Amélie kissed Nino, then kisses the side of my neck, the way Amélie also kissed Nino, then right above my eye, the way Amélie kissed Nino too, which makes me laugh and has him looking at me expectantly, so I do the same. The corner of his mouth. His neck—I let my fingers touch his collarbone, and that hollow—I want to kiss it too, but I have to finish first, so I kiss right above his eye and feel his eyelashes against my chin.

I sit back, and we just look at each other.

"I really like you, Bird," Ollie says. He wraps his arms around me, and I hold him to me also—try to focus on his body against mine, his chest and heartbeat thumping right alongside my own. Try not to think of how I won't be able to hold him like this again when it ends.

16

THE BENCHES ARE DAMP WHEN I GET TO SCHOOL. OLLIE IS standing outside, talking to Florence and Ashley—and shit, I know I should already be past this. But walking over feels like such a bad idea. Flo, the girl who I used to be with and still love, speaking to Ollie, the boy I am currently with and also love.

I take a breath and make my way over. Ashley sees me first and waves, and Flo turns and grins. I don't usually get this kind of welcome. I'm not sure what Oliver James has or hasn't already said. I haven't talked this through with Ollie yet—if he's all right with other people knowing. If *I'm* all right with other people knowing.

Ollie's cheeks turn a little red as I reach the three of them.

"Sorry. The news sort of . . . spilled."

Between Ash and Flo's expert interrogation techniques, I'm not surprised they got the truth out of him.

Ashley points at us. "You two are officially the cutest couple in the school."

"Don't worry," Florence says. "We won't tell anyone if you don't want us to."

"Tell anyone what?" Gideon asks, walking up from behind me. He slings an arm over my shoulder.

I hesitate, but Ollie shrugs.

"They made it official," Flo says, apparently already forgetting her promise.

Gideon starts to smirk. "No shit—really?"

The bell rings, and Florence hooks arms with Ollie, walking ahead while Gideon follows. Ashley lingers behind, arms wrapped around herself, and though she doesn't make eye contact, there's clearly something she wants to say.

"You guys are cute," Ashley says, walking beside me.

I rub the back of my neck. "Thanks. I guess."

She lets out a breath and plays with the ends of her hair. "I need to talk to you."

"Okay." I pause. "Is something wrong?"

"What? No," she says. "I just—I don't know. I guess I was inspired." She glances at me. "By you and Ollie."

I squint at her.

"I guess—I realized I might be missing out on something,

and I don't want to be," she says, then pauses as she stops walking to face me. "I have a secret to tell you, but you can't tell anyone."

I glance away. "Okay . . ."

"Seriously—you can't tell anyone, Bird."

"All right, I won't."

She takes a deep breath. "I have a crush on Gideon."

She's watching me expectantly, so I widen my eyes. "Oh, wow. That's—uh—huge."

She keeps walking. "I know. He has no idea."

That might be accurate, at least.

"I've been thinking . . . Maybe I should tell him. I'll never really know what'll happen until I do it, right?"

I can't help but smile a little. "Yeah, that's true."

"Could you help me?" she asks. "I want to figure out a way to tell him that'll really catch his attention."

I let out a little laugh before I realize she's being 100 percent serious. "Oh."

Her feelings seem a little hurt. "Never mind, it was a stupid idea—"

"No, wait—Ashley. Yeah, of course I'll help."

She breaks out into a smile before hooking her arm with mine and guiding me toward the doors. "Seriously, congratulations," she says. "I'm really happy for you and Oliver James."

"Thanks, Ash."

* * *

A few weeks pass, and I realize how easy it is to get used to a new normal. Oliver James Hernández is my boyfriend. My arm's healed and the cast comes off. My skin is yellow in comparison to the brown around it. It's a little gross, but I just make sure to keep it covered with long sleeves.

Nothing really changes between me and Ollie. We still do everything we always have, just with more kissing. I go over to his place to "watch movies" and we always end up making out, the laptop shut off and on the floor. Sometimes the shirts come off, but that's about as far as we go.

Sometimes we talk about the contest. Ollie just needs to put ten more photos into his portfolio, but he takes hundreds of me, looking for the perfect ones. He stages me in his room, my shirt off, and I hope to God no one else is going to see these pictures, because it'd be pretty effing embarrassing if someone did.

I haven't been to film club in a while, and Ollie says he wants to come too, but Flo says she has too much homework and leaves the two of us behind with a little smirk. I'm going to have to kill her privately later.

Now that it's pretty close to Halloween, the film club moderator gives us *Pan's Labyrinth* to watch with its English subtitles—my tenth favorite movie of all time. It's not really a horror, but it's still got some of the scariest shit I've seen. The Pale Man, with the freaking eyes—those freaking eyes, man— gave me nightmares for weeks when I first saw it. Granted,

I was six, and my dad thought it was a kids' movie when he popped it in the DVD player and left the room, running back in at the end when I wouldn't stop screaming—but still.

The movie starts, and even though we're all in our snuggle pile, it's still creepy with the lights turned off. The popcorn gets stuck on one side of the room, and no one even cares. Even Theo and Winona have stopped making out to stare up at the ceiling with these horrified expressions, and someone won't stop whispering, "Oh shit. Oh shit."

I'm super still next to Ollie. A man and his son insist they've only been hunting on the screen. I close my eyes, knowing what's coming. The movie's pretty gory. This may be one of my favorites, but I've never been into watching bloody films—have never had the stomach for it. The Pale Man comes on, and my childhood traumas make my heart beat faster. I squeeze my eyes shut.

Ollie's arm presses against mine. I turn to look at him, and he leans closer. "Are you okay?"

I nod.

"We don't have to stay if you don't want to," he says. "We can get out of here. If you want to, anyway."

"Bird," Theo hisses. "Tell your boyfriend to shut up."

I point at myself, bring my hands toward my chest, point a *V* from my eyes and up at the ceiling. "It's okay. I want to watch."

Ollie nods. Our arms are still up against each other's. His

skin is hot, and our arms are close enough that I can feel his fingers twitch against mine every time they move. I don't look at him for the rest of the movie.

"Holy shit," someone whispers.

The credits roll. Everyone looks a little shell-shocked and gray when the lights flash on. The cold popcorn is thrown out. We all stumble outside. It's even darker out now that it's October, the light purple with streaks of red across the sky, and the fall chill feels a little icier. Every little movement in the trees and the shadows looks creepy as hell. People hang around before going home, but Ollie and I start our walk back.

I hand him my phone. **Maybe watching that was a bad idea. Definitely going to have nightmares tonight.**

Ollie gives me a sympathetic smile as he hands the phone back. "Do you want to come over?" he asks. "Stay the night?"

I almost stop walking. I've come over plenty of times, and we typically end up making out . . . but I always leave before we can get really into it—say I have curfew, throw on my shirt, and practically run out the door. I'm a little scared of what might happen if I end up staying any longer than I usually do.

I hand him my phone. **That's okay. I'll be all right.**

He shrugs. "Okay. Let me know if you change your mind."

We walk in silence for a while. It's not like I don't want to go over. I do. I'm pretty freaked out, and I don't want to be alone right now. Besides that, I *like* Oliver James—want to spend time with him whenever I can. Maybe going over doesn't necessarily mean having sex.

I give him my phone again. **Actually, yeah, it'd be great if I could stay over. Let me just ask my mom.**

He nods, watching as I text. My mom doesn't know about me or Ollie—if she did, her answer would be no. She takes a second to respond.

Ollie says, "Sorry you're so freaked out."

I shrug. "I knew it was an effed-up movie. I guess I'm kind of traumatized from seeing it as a kid."

My mom texts back that it's fine.

Oliver pokes my arm, smiling a little, like he thinks my inability to watch horror movies is funny—or cute. "Are you going to be all right?"

I hadn't really been looking at him, because I'm pretty nervous about what'll happen when I get to his place and don't have the excuse of curfew to leave—but I look at him now, and his steady gaze, stable in who he is, makes me feel a little more secure.

I smile. "Yeah. I'll be okay."

We get to Ollie's pretty quickly, walking fast to escape the creepy-ass dark where every shadow looks like the Pale Man lurking behind a tree. Ollie takes my hand, like he's been doing more and more lately, and my heart starts hammering in my throat. I have a feeling about how tonight's going to go, and I don't know if I'm ready for it.

The lights are off when we get to his house. Ollie's mom

already left for her class. Donna Noble bounds up against us when we come in the front door, her tail wagging furiously before she sits back to watch us walk down the hall. We get into his bedroom, and Oliver closes the door behind me with a snap that echoes.

Ollie unbuttons his sweater, hangs it up in his closet. "Do you want to watch videos or something?" he says, dragging his laptop to his bed.

We start re-watching *Doctor Who* from the beginning, and look at *Heroes* when we agree that Rose can be just a little annoying sometimes, and when we've had enough of Claire, he just scrolls through BuzzFeed with the Lorde Pandora station on, playing a little louder than anyone else usually would this late at night. His leg started out as touching mine, but by the time he switches from Lorde to Santigold, his hand is on my knee, absentmindedly moving its way up and down. If he sees the very hard result of him stroking my leg, he doesn't seem to care. It's midnight now.

He glances at me. "It's getting late. Want to go to bed?"

I swallow and nod.

Ollie smiles and lands a quick peck on my lips before he puts his laptop back onto his desk and closes it, cutting Purity Ring off mid-stream. He starts fiddling with the sheets, looking up at me through his eyelashes. I forget to breathe.

"I can sleep on the couch," I tell him, but Ollie gives me a look.

"Why would you do that?"

I get into bed while he plays with his phone for a second, not looking at me, and I see he's setting his vibration alarm. He gets off the bed and crosses the room to turn off the lights, throwing us into a pale dark, his silvery blue night-light glowing in the corner of the room. Ollie rustles with the sheets and climbs into bed beside me again.

It's legitimately painful, just lying there next to him. I can hear him breathing, feel him lying still, like he's trying his best not to move—like he's super aware of the fact that this is my first time spending the night since we were kids also, and he knows exactly how this will play out if we start messing around—and I guess I understand, because I'm trying not to move too.

Ollie rolls over beside me so that he's on his side, looking at me. "Could we . . ." he starts, then stops himself.

Seriously, it's amazing I haven't had a heart attack yet.

He rolls onto his back again. "Can we snuggle?"

That's not at all what I was expecting him to say. We've cuddled loads of times—usually right before making out. But I get why he's being weird about it. My body (i.e., my dick) screams at me to just say yes, there's no reason to even hesitate, just say YES. But the word gets stuck in my throat, and the silence hits such new levels of awkwardness that the craziness of it all just makes me laugh. Ollie notices and looks at me with a smile, grabs his phone and turns on his flashlight so that the room becomes a bright blue, his brown eyes and dimples shining. "What?"

I shake my head, still laughing. I tap my temple, shaking my head. "I don't know. This is just weird."

His gaze drops, and I wave my hand so he looks back up at me.

"No, not you. I mean—just everything. Fuck. I mean, fuck it. Yeah—come here."

He grins and turns off the flashlight, lies down with his head on my chest, his hair tickling my neck, and he feels so good there.

He buries his head into my chest, and my arms hold him tightly, hand going up and down his back. His leg presses in between my legs, and I know he can feel what's going on there—but he doesn't move away, just adjusts himself so I can feel what's going on with him too, and legs and hips start moving in that automatic way they do, and he lets out this little sound that just about kills me.

He starts to lean forward, still looking at me tentatively—like he wants to make sure this is okay. I could push him away. I could tell him to stop. But I don't. His mouth is on mine—slow at first, then harder, lips opening, and I pull him closer, pressing against him while he's on top of me—and shit, I know this isn't a good idea. I know this can't end well.

He pulls his mouth away and looks at me, gaze flitting across my face. Pulls his hands out from beneath my shirt to put his fingers in my hair. "You okay?"

I nod.

I'm not sure he believes me. "Is it okay if I keep going?"

I nod again.

That's what he does, his mouth moving down my neck, my chest, my stomach, his hands wrestling with my jeans until he gets them unbuttoned and unzipped, tugs them down, laughs when they get stuck at my feet. He stops laughing, just grins at me as he leans down to kiss me again, his hands sliding beneath my boxers, smiling against my mouth as I fumble with his jeans, struggle to get them off too, until mini-Oliver and mini-Nathan are pressing up against each other, and Ollie's not smiling against my mouth anymore—he's breathing hard, making enough noise that I'm really freaking happy that his mother's out of the house, especially since I'm being just as loud, if not louder. He lets go of me, and before I can even mourn the loss, his mouth is on me, and my hands are in his curls, my back lifting off his bed, his hands tugging me up and deeper into his mouth, and holy shit, we've never done this before and I feel like I'm about to come instantly, which would be humiliating—

Ollie pulls up suddenly, breathing hard, and he's giving me that look that I'm starting to get a little more used to seeing as he signs something that I don't understand.

"What?"

He says it out loud. "I really want you."

It's kind of obvious what he means. I know I want him too—want to know what it feels like with him, want to get rid of all the space in between us, and at that thought alone my heart feels like it's about to implode—but I hesitate.

I can't actually believe I'm doing this again, but I pull back. "I don't know."

"I can't see what you're saying," he tells me, so I grab his phone and swipe on the flashlight again.

"I think we should stop."

He looks surprised—and a little hurt.

"I mean," I quickly say, "I want to. Holy fuck, I want to."

He's watching me, more intensely than he ever has, waiting for me to speak.

"But I . . ." I feel like I could slap myself. "I don't think I'm ready."

He bites the corner of his lip and nods. "We don't have to right now."

"Okay."

"But I want to eventually," he says.

Eventually. I take a breath. I know that I want to. I'd be lying to myself if I said I didn't. But I also know it's going to be awkward. What if it's so bad that Ollie decides he doesn't want anything else to do with me?

Ollie keeps speaking. "I guess we should look it up anyway. Do some research or something."

I hesitate. "So—you haven't done this before?"

He shakes his head with a slow-growing smile and kisses me again, this time without the same kind of frenzy we had before—kisses and moves his hands over me slowly, and I try matching his gentleness, until we're moving against each other, his face buried in my neck, me gasping in his ear, until his sheets are messed up and we just lie there together. We grab tissues from a box of Kleenex and wipe ourselves down. Ollie grabs his camera from his desk and plays around, straddling me and everything and snapping photos while I try to hide my face, both of us laughing just a little too loudly, until he puts the camera down and we end up going for another round.

We wake up with the sun shining bright, haul on our clothes, brush teeth, untangle hair, and get out the door. We walk to school without really saying anything. Ollie keeps looking at me—like maybe he's a little worried.

"Is everything okay?" he asks.

I nod. "Yeah. Everything's fine."

He looks like he doesn't really believe me, and I can't blame him, because I don't really believe myself. Last night was good. Really effing good. But now we've broached the subject I've been trying to avoid, and I know there's no turning back.

Ollie walks beside me in the school hallway. He asks, "Did I push you into anything you didn't really want to do?"

It's embarrassing he's even bringing it up. I give him my phone. **No. You definitely didn't push me into anything.**

"Are you sure?"

I nod. "Yeah. I'm sure."

"We don't have to—you know, have sex if you don't want to."

I know that—or I'm supposed to know it, anyway. But I feel trapped in a corner. Last time I didn't have sex with Florence, it felt like I kind of ruined everything between us. But if I have sex with Ollie, that might ruin everything anyway.

"Yeah. I know. I want to."

He smiles and takes my hand, and we keep walking down the hall together.

17

MY MOM'S SITTING IN THE LIVING ROOM, IN HER FAVORITE spot on the couch. She has her feet up on the center table, flipping through channels. I almost slip by to run up the stairs to my room, to keep writing—the deadline is a little over a month away now, and I'm only about halfway through the script—but as I hit the first few stairs, I realize my mom didn't even bother trying to call me over. I slow to a stop. Backtrack. Plop down on the sofa beside her.

She looks pleasantly surprised. "You're back earlier than usual."

I decide to be perfectly honest. "I wanted to get home to write."

She purses her lips and doesn't say anything to that.

"Isn't *Friends* on?"

"It was an episode I've seen a few times now. The one where Joey and Chandler get robbed."

We sit quietly for a while.

"Mom?"

She turns to me, waiting. I didn't really mean to bring this up now—but I've been thinking a lot about everything Ollie said to me. The idea that I have to write, no matter what. It's still ringing through me.

"I wanted to talk to you about that contest."

She sighs. "Nate—"

"No, just hear me out. Please."

She crosses her arms and waits.

"I know I probably won't win anyway. And I know you're worried about me going across the country. But . . . I want to try. Need to try."

She stares at the TV with her arms still crossed. This isn't looking good. "I really don't know, Nate. I have to think about it."

That's a big step up from an outright *no*, but I decide to push my luck. "What's there to think about? I'd get to take classes for free, a stipend of two thousand dollars, and free room and board—"

"And the plane ticket? What about money for supplies, textbooks?" She sighs again. "It's just a lot to think about. New York isn't exactly safe."

I shake my head. "Why're you like this?" I know I should stop, and the warning look she gives me is confirmation, but I keep going anyway. "I know Dad died, but you act like you think you're going to lose me, too. All of these rules, and the curfew, and now I can't apply—"

Her voice gets louder. "You can still write without applying for summer college classes."

I should shut up, but I just keep going. "It's like—I don't know, like Dad is dead and Becca went to college and you don't want to be left alone, so you're holding on to me, but you can't do that forever. I have to be able to leave. I have to live my own life without worrying about you all of the time—without feeling sorry for you."

The silence. There aren't any words to describe it. My mom's looking at me, and I think her eyes are wet, and I'm officially the spoiled, crappiest son in the world who made his mother cry. I don't even know what to say to make it better again. I'm not sure there's anything that I can say.

She gets up and leaves, walking up the stairs. I shut off the TV and go to my room and end up lying around in bed, watching Netflix with the volume super low, trying not to think about everything I said, but of course unable to think about anything else.

The things I said to my mother are still echoing in my head by the time I meet with Ollie on the corner; and by lunch,

I've moved on to hating myself for being the piece-of-shit kid who treats his own mom like trash. I'm walking through the courtyard, past the damp benches and toward the greenhouse, when someone grabs my arm. I spin around to find Ashley. Her face is red and her eyes are wide.

"Jesus, Ash, you scared the shit out of me."

"Did you forget what day it is?"

I stare at her blankly until the realization hits me. *Shit.* "No—no, of course I didn't forget."

"You forgot."

"All right, maybe a little."

She dances from one foot to the next nervously. "I don't think I can do this."

I put my hands on her shoulders. "You can. You will. Gideon's going to love it." I think I might be trying to convince myself, too.

"Maybe this isn't a good idea."

I try to ignore the part of me that's a little scared for her also. "You'll be great. Look—he's sitting over there."

Gideon's on benches with the soccer team, laughing loudly. Ashley and I exchange looks, and I swear to God it's like I'm the one who's about to make a complete fool of myself for the sake of love, my heart's beating so hard. She takes a deep breath, reaches into her bag, pulls out the sign, and leaps onto one of the courtyard benches.

"Gideon Roth," she shouts—only it comes out more like

a yelp. Her voice breaks, and only a few freshmen walking by glance at her, giving her weird looks. I'm starting to see that maybe this isn't the best idea after all, but before I can say anything, she clears her throat. "GIDEON ROTH!"

Heads swivel. Conversations stop. Gideon stares up at Ashley with a confused look on his face.

"Ash?" he says, his voice sounding small across the courtyard. "What're you doing?"

Ashley takes another deep breath, and I feel myself holding my own. "I've been trying to find the right words to express just how I feel about you, and nothing felt right, because I realized I can't just say it. I've had a crush on you since we were in elementary school together and you asked to borrow my eraser, and I still feel the same way now. Gideon, I have something to ask you." She holds up a huge red sign made of paper, decorated with origami flowers that she clearly spent hours on. The words WILL YOU BE MY BOYFRIEND, GIDEON ROTH? are carefully stenciled across in silver and gold glitter.

Everyone in the courtyard stares at Ashley, then turns to look at Gideon for his reaction. He lets out a laugh, like he thinks she's joking. It lasts for just a second—more like a nervous tic than anything else—but it's enough. The soccer team starts cracking up all around him, and half the courtyard follows. Ashley's cheeks are as red as the sign, and without a word she leaps from the bench, turns on her heel, and races from the courtyard, sign still wobbling in her hands. People make the *ooooooooh* sound. Florence—I didn't even see her watching, don't know where she came from—hurries after Ashley without sparing me a glance. Gideon makes eye contact with me across the courtyard. He looks just as shell-shocked as I feel.

I'd told Ashley to try a grand gesture. I'd seen enough epic videos of guys and girls asking each other out, and it always seemed like grand gestures worked in movies. Boombox high above the head, singing "Can't Take My Eyes Off of You" to the tune of a marching band, making out on the pitcher's mound in front of a crowd . . . But those were movies. I should've realized that wouldn't have worked in real life.

Gideon gets up, still laughing along with his friends, rolling his eyes and grinning—but when he crosses over to me, his smile disappears. "What the hell?" he says beneath his breath. "Did you put Ashley up to that?"

I kind of did, but I don't want to admit to that now.

"What—was it a prank or something?"

I stare at him blankly. "No—no, Gideon, Ashley was really telling you how she felt."

He looks confused. "Why would she do that?"

I look away, pretty confused myself. "I mean—because she likes you. . . ."

"But *why?*"

I'm not sure what to say to that. "Look, I think she was pretty hurt—"

"And whose fault is that?" he says defensively. "It sure as hell isn't mine."

I want to point out that his first instinct was to laugh at Ashley, but he's also right—I made her think everything would be okay. She might've wanted to tell Gideon in a way that would stand out, but announcing it in front of half the school was *my* idea. "You really never knew that Ash had feelings for you?"

He's frowning. "I mean, sometimes I wondered, I guess."

"And you don't—I don't know, feel anything for Ashley?"

He shrugs. "I never really thought about it."

"Maybe now's a good time to start thinking about it."

He doesn't say anything as I turn away, jogging down the path Ashley and Florence took. I get to the greenhouse, but when I open the door, Florence looks up at me and points. "Out. Get out."

"I just—" I don't even know what I'm going to say, but all words leave my mouth when I see Ashley crying at one of the benches, Ollie rubbing one of her arms.

"No, I don't care. Get out—now, Bird!"

I turn and leave, the door swinging shut behind me.

The rest of the school day goes by without me really talking to anyone else. I'm not sure if I'm in just as much trouble as Gideon, but I feel a little better when I see Ollie waiting for me on the benches. We begin the walk home in silence. At first he just talks about a hard quiz he'd had earlier in physics, but I ask how Ashley is doing, and he looks like he'd been hoping I wasn't going to bring her up.

He shrugs. "I don't know. She's fine, I guess. Or will be fine."

I pass him my phone. **I don't know what happened. I really thought it was going to work.**

He looks at me like it should be obvious. "I mean, it's kind of embarrassing. Not everyone wants to be put on the spot like that in front of the whole school."

I sigh. **I feel like shit. I helped her come up with the idea.**

He takes my hand. "Well, you could help her come up with a better one." He stares off in front of us, and he seems a little distracted, so I squeeze his hand so that he'll look at me.

"Is everything all right?"

He doesn't answer for a second. "I spoke to my dad," he says. "I told him I think I might want to stay in Seattle after all, but he still wants me to move back. I don't think he'll make me, but—I don't know. I figured he would let it go."

The thought of losing Ollie now—I stop in my tracks. He turns to face me.

"I'm sorry," he says. "I shouldn't have brought it up. It's not a big deal. I promise."

I'm not sure if I believe him, but it's clear from his expression that he doesn't want to talk about it anymore, so we keep walking.

* * *

I find Ashley in the hallway before homeroom the next day. I try to wave for her attention, but she pretends she doesn't see me, speeding up her walk, books held tightly to her chest. I hurry after her, jogging to keep pace.

"Ashley," I say, but she won't look at me. I decide to just keep going. "I'm really sorry. I didn't know it was going to end up that way."

"Really?" she says, finally glancing at me. "It's a little hard to tell. Maybe you wanted to humiliate me in front of the entire school."

"Why would I want that?"

She slows to a stop, looks up at me with red eyes. "Because everyone thinks I'm a joke? Who'd want to seriously date Ashley Perkins, right?"

I'm shaking my head. "No one thinks you're a joke."

She considers me for a second before looking away. "That's what it feels like."

"You decided to tell Gideon because you wanted to see what'd happen. There's nothing wrong with that."

She takes a breath and looks like she's going to start crying, and the asshole in me hopes that she doesn't because I wouldn't really be sure what to do—but she only nods. "Yeah. You're right. I'm just looking for someone to be mad at besides myself."

"Don't be mad at yourself. I'd rather you be mad at me than mad at yourself."

She smiles. "Okay, I'll be mad at you, then."

The bell's about to ring, so we keep walking. "Have you spoken to Gideon yet?" I ask.

"Not face-to-face," she tells me. "He texted me last night saying he didn't feel the same way, but he was flattered." She shrugs, like it isn't a big deal, even though we both know it is. "You were right, Bird. It was worth a shot."

Florence decides she misses our draw-on-my-arm sessions, and to be honest, I kind of miss them too, so I grab my bike and pedal to Flo's place, walk through the front door, and wait for Tobey Maguire to finish his humping. Florence leads me up to her room, and I realize it's been a while since I came over. I feel a spark of guilt about that.

"So, Bird," she says, pen twirling in her hand. "What should I draw for you tonight?"

"Oh, I don't know," I say, flopping onto her bed. Ethel blinks at me from the pillow. "Surprise me."

"I know just the thing."

Ethel stretches and wanders over, rubbing against my arm. I scratch her chin, but she shakes her head and leaps from the bed. I let out a breath and close my eyes. "Shit's been crazy, Flo."

"I know," she says, glancing at me over the rims of her glasses. "Attempting to play matchmaker can be stressful."

I rub my face. "I really fucked up."

"Yeah," she says, "but at least you apologized."

I feel a twinge. There's someone else I owe an apology—but my mom and I have been avoiding each other. I have a feeling we'll keep avoiding each other until I find the courage to actually face the bullshit I told her.

Florence draws in silence for another second, her pen scratching against the paper.

"I should be focusing on things with me and Ollie," I tell her.

"Everything okay?" she asks without looking up.

"Well," I start, unsure if I even want to tell her—it's more than a little embarrassing to say out loud, but I soldier on. "Ollie and I were thinking of . . . you know."

She puts down her pen and swivels in her chair to face me. "You're thinking about it, are you?"

I clear my throat. "Well, we talked about it."

She grins, but she won't meet my eye. "I'm happy for you, whatever you decide."

I rub the back of my neck. "Thanks, Flo." She goes back to drawing, smile now stuck on her face. "I'm sorry about yesterday."

"You don't need to keep apologizing," she says. "At least, not to me. It was a sweet intention, but had horrible execution."

"Do you think they'll be all right?"

Her pen slows down. "I don't know. Ashley was really embarrassed, and Gideon's so oblivious to how she's feeling, it's hard to know what's going through his head."

"Shit. I hope I haven't screwed up their friendship."

She glances at me. "They'll be fine. We figured it out, right?"

Depends on the definition of *figured it out*, I guess.

"I know I've said this before, but seriously—I'm happy for you and Ollie," she says.

I roll my eyes.

"No, really—it's okay to be happy for you two, right? Now," she says, "I just need to work on finding the love of my life."

That sends a pang through me. I thought I'd be the love of her life, once upon a time. But it'd be stupid to think that she should wait for me, or that she can't be with anyone else. If she wants to find the love of her life—then that's what I want for her too. I sit up. "You'll find someone."

"Oh, I know," she says, giving me a look. "I'm way too amazing for someone to *not* fall in love with me. Lydia's been texting," she says. "She told me she wants to be friends." She puts air quotes around "friends."

"Do you want to be?" I ask.

"Definitely not. That's the end. I'm cutting her off. No more Lydia."

"Good. I'm glad."

She gets quiet, focusing on her drawing, so I sit still and listen to her Pandora station and think about how much really has changed in just a few months, and how things probably will keep changing over the next few years, too. The thought that everything keeps changing used to give me a shit ton of anxiety—but now I'm realizing that's just exactly who I am: a guy who's going to keep evolving. And maybe that's okay.

Florence finishes her drawing. She passes it over to me.

"Is this your self-portrait?" I ask, which is stupid, because it's so obviously her.

"Yes," Flo says, swinging her silvery-purple twists over her shoulder. "And you should be grateful, too. That'll look nice up on your wall, and you'll get to see me all of the time now."

I laugh and shake my head, and she grins and kisses my cheek, before we get on to talking nonstop, about nothing, just about bullshit, the way we always have.

18

TIME PASSES BY, LIKE IT ALWAYS SEEMS TO DO, UNTIL IT'S the night of Gideon's annual Halloween party of drunken revelry. I get permission from my mom to go, since it's on a Friday, and it's only once a year. It's basically the obligatory scene in any teen film: he's rich as hell, so I ride my bike up toward the Highlands, where there's more space in between the front yards, and the houses are two stories higher than any of the ones on my street. Gideon's house has its own private gravel driveway. Even from outside I can hear the music blasting and thumping through the ground along with the screams and laughter.

The hallways are packed and there's the sickly sweet scent of spiked fruit punch and maybe a little vomit too, and the living room has people jumping up and down and screaming the words to a song while Theo and Winona make out in their personal corner. Too many people, not enough space. I'm a little too much of a classic introvert to even be here, but I always end up coming, since I know Florence and Ashley will freak out if I don't.

I end up downstairs in the basement with its brick walls and the bar, where I usually find Ash and Gideon with Flo every year, but this time there are just familiar faces from different classes, Emma and Lucas nodding their heads and smiling at me. I turn back upstairs again and hop up the staircase to the next floor, when someone grabs my shoulder and shoves me so hard that I almost trip. I steady myself and whirl around to see a door slamming in my face. I step forward, try the knob—it's locked.

"Nate?"

I turn, and Ollie is standing up from the edge of a bed. The room practically looks like a hotel suite, or one of those bedrooms designed just for magazines. Everything's in its perfect place, and it's clear we really shouldn't be in here.

Ollie puts his hands to his chest, brings them up with a small shrug. "What's going on?"

Crap. I try the knob again, then pound on the door. "What the fuck? Let us out!"

I hear laughter from the other side. Gideon and Ashley. I'm guessing their friendship is going to be just effing fine.

"You've got to be kidding me," I say, still pounding on the door.

"You two really need to talk," Ash's muffled voice comes through the wood. Her words are slurring. I'm pretty sure this is the first time Ashley's ever been drunk. "We'll let you out when you're done."

I keep pounding on the door, but I already know Ashley's dead serious. She'll probably just keep us locked in here until the party's over and our parents have reported us missing.

Ollie's already sat down on the edge of the bed—probably picked up on the clue that we've been locked inside as a joke. He shrugs—like he doesn't mind if he's locked in here for the rest of eternity. Crap. The thought alone is enough to make me feel like having a panic attack.

"Shit. I'm sorry about this."

"Who locked us in? Gideon?"

"And Ashley, yeah."

He looks a little surprised, and I get it. Gideon, sure—he can be an asshole. But Ash?

I pass him my phone. **She said we need to talk.**

Ollie cringes a little, looking away with some guilt, and I realize that I may not have a clue—but he knows exactly what's going on. I pause, waiting, until he says, "I might've spoken to her a little more about—well, you know, what we've been thinking about doing. . . ."

I don't know what to say. I don't know what to do. I grab my phone back from him, hold up the screen. **You've been talking to Ashley Perkins about whether we're going to have sex or not?**

He glances up at me. "Well, when you put it that way—"

I roll my eyes and turn my back to him. He gets up and walks toward me with shuffling footsteps. "I'm sorry. After the whole thing with Gideon, we were talking, and she asked me how things were going, and I—I don't know, I just wanted some advice—"

I turn back to face him, holding up my phone again. **That shit's personal, Ollie. Private. I don't need anyone else knowing about us like that.**

"You're right. I'm sorry."

"Freaking Ashley Perkins? She'll never shut up about it."

Ollie frowns, but he doesn't say anything.

I shake my head, type on my phone again. **Why would you go to her? If you need to talk about something, why not just come to me?**

His eyes scan the phone and he shrugs a little. "I don't know. You're a little sensitive—"

"*Sensitive?*"

"Nervous," he says quickly, "about all of this, and I don't want to freak you out even more, so I just went to her to have someone to talk to, since I couldn't really talk to you about it, and she ended up giving me pretty good advice."

I bite my bottom lip, look away. "And what'd she have to say?"

He takes a step closer. "To let you take the lead."

I raise my eyebrows.

"She suggested it might make you more nervous if I'm the one bringing it up—like I'm pressuring you or something. I don't mean to pressure you." He takes my hand, and I have to force myself to let him. "I'm ready whenever you are—and if you're never ready, that's okay, too."

I search his face, and I can see he really, 100 percent means it. I take my hand away, search for the right words, hand him my phone. **I'm not sure when I'll be ready. I'm just so worried that doing it will ruin everything.**

He frowns. "Why would it ruin everything?"

"What if I suck?"

He laughs. "That might not be a bad thing." My mouth falls open, but he just keeps grinning. "The first time probably isn't going to be great. Every article and website I read pretty much said so. They said—" and he adds something here, but I'm not sure what, sounds blending together. "But if I'm going to experience it, I want to have that experience with you."

It takes me a while to respond. **You read articles and websites about it?**

He shrugs. "I wanted to be prepared."

We sit on the edge of the bed. I hold my hands tightly together.

"If it's not great," he says, "we can try again, and keep trying until it does get good. And if it never does, maybe that's okay too. We're not in a relationship just to have sex."

"Christ, how'd you get so smart about this kind of stuff?"

"I did a lot of reading."

I glance at him, and he's watching like he's waiting for me to say something, do something, and the words are there—I just have to say them. "I'm ready."

He crosses his index and middle finger and extends them from his lips, points at me, extends his index finger from his mouth again. "Are you sure?"

No, I'm not sure at all. But I nod, because I know I'll always be nervous, and Ollie's right—there isn't anyone else I'd want to experience this with either. He leans forward, kisses me, and I realize that Ashley and Gideon might've locked me in this room with Ollie just so that we could have sex right here and now. We fall down onto the bed together, and this—the kissing, the hands beneath shirts, the fingers fumbling with zippers—this I'm familiar with, comfortable with, but it's when Ollie sits up and tells me it'll take some preparation that my heart starts to hammer against my chest.

I guess he sees my nervousness. "We don't have to do this tonight. Maybe we should wait until—"

I hear muffled shouting. The door bursts open. The shouting fills the room, and Florence marches inside. "That's fucked up and you know it!"

Ashley quickly follows, twisting her hands. "We were just trying to help."

"You're a mean drunk," Flo accuses, pointing a finger in

Ashley's face. She spins to me. "I'm sorry, Bird, I didn't know what they were planning—"

She stops. Sees the situation. Ollie's face is a deep red as he jumps up and yanks back on his shirt, and I sit up and tug my pants back on. Ashley looks positively radiant. She beams at me and tries to tug Florence out the door, but I say it's all right. The mood's been killed—there's no way I'll be able to keep going, knowing that everyone on the other side of the door is trying to listen in. And besides, maybe this *isn't* the best place to do this for the first time. Oliver shares a look with me, like he understands and agrees, and we follow Florence and Ashley out, telling them repeatedly that it's okay, they weren't interrupting anything at all.

Most people have left before the sun starts to rise. Only a few of us are lying around in Gideon's backyard. Gideon is nowhere to be seen, and Ash is having a deep, heartfelt conversation with Ollie. They're sitting up, cross-legged, holding each other's hands. I'm a little worried about what Ash might be drunkenly telling him, but Flo tells me not to worry.

"She can be a mean drunk, but I don't think she'll tell him anything he doesn't already know."

I can only hope she's right. Florence lies down beside me, and I rest one hand behind my head as we stare up at the layer of clouds turning pink and gold.

"This is really beautiful," she says.

"Yeah." The clouds are beautiful, the sunrise is beautiful, and I need to get over myself—need to stop being in my head all the damn time. Need to stop glancing over at Ollie, who is now laughing so hard that his cheeks have turned red.

Florence glances over at Ash and Ollie, also. They're hugging—well, it's more like Ash is squeezing the life out of Oliver, who looks like he might need some help, but when he catches our eyes he only waves at us. Flo waves back. She turns to me.

"Listen. I know that Ashley can be a little Amy Poehler–insane sometimes. But I'm with her."

"What do you mean?"

"I'm really happy for you. Overjoyed, in fact. I mean, this is kind of an epic love story."

I can't help but laugh. "What do you mean? There's nothing epic about it."

"Well, I mean. I guess you're not stuck in an arena fighting to the death for each other, or taking down a government or an evil wizard."

"No. No, we're not doing any of that."

"But that's what makes it epic. You don't need to die for each other to make this exciting. Just the fact that you're here, together—that's enough. That's epic enough."

She makes me smile, despite myself. "Thanks, Flo."

"No problem, Bird. Let's bring it in."

"Oh, come on. Seriously?"

"Yes. This is always serious."

I sigh and put my hand on top of hers.

"Clear eyes. Full hearts. Can't lose." She grins as she lies back down, and I can't stop smiling either when I lie back down beside her.

19

OLLIE TELLS ME THAT HE WANTS TO TAKE MORE PHOTO-graphs of me, so I end up walking the walk up the hill to his house, but I'm nervous as hell, because I'm pretty sure the next time we're alone together we're going to have sex, so I'm a little scared right now. Okay. More than a little scared. Freaking the fuck out.

The front door is left unlocked for me. His mom is in the living room, sitting comfortably in front of the TV with Ollie and Donna Noble. Mrs. Hernández smiles at me like she knows everything about me and her son, which is a little embarrassing. It's going to take some getting used to the fact that we're boyfriends. Boyfriend and boyfriend. The step before ex-boyfriend and ex-boyfriend.

"What're the plans for tonight?" she asks pointedly, hands flying through the air. Ollie doesn't seem to have seen her ask the question—either that, or he's purposely ignoring her.

"Uh—movies," I say. "Netflix. The usual."

She squints at me, like she can totally tell I'm planning on having sex with her son. "Well, whatever you do, make sure that you stay *safe*," she says, landing her gaze on Oliver.

Ollie definitely saw that time—his ears get red. "Got it, Mom. Thanks."

Mrs. Hernández gives Oliver James a quick hug before leaving for her night class, and when Ollie closes the door behind him, he bites his lip. I follow him into his room, where he has me sit on his bed. His walls are covered with photos he's taken now. It's like his bedroom has transformed into a gallery. I could stare at his photos all day, because he's pretty amazing—probably really will end up a famous photographer one day.

"Bird," he says, setting up his camera, watching my face through the viewfinder. "You still look nervous."

"I guess I am."

"Why? I don't make you nervous, do I?"

"Maybe a little."

Ollie looks up from the camera. "I don't mean to make you nervous."

"I know. You're not doing anything. It's just me."

He looks back to the viewfinder, snaps a photo—then

suddenly looks up from his camera again and puts it down on his desk and walks over to me and the bed. He's smiling a little, like he thinks my nervousness is cute. But he also has that intense look in his eye. I ask him if he wants to watch a movie with me, and he says yes, like he knows exactly what I'm doing—trying to avoid why I'm here. I choose *The Matrix* (third favorite movie of all time) from Ollie's list of down-loaded movies, except that I don't really watch it, because I can't stop glancing over at Ollie—can't stop looking at the expressions that flash across his face. Intensity, a smile, sur-prise, as his eyes scan over the screen and the captions.

At some point, sitting up becomes uncomfortable, and Ollie must notice me shifting and trying to wake up one of my legs, which has fallen asleep and has thousands of needles running through it, because he presses his palms downward, telling me to relax. I lie down next to him, and we end up a lot closer than necessary, our shoulders touching, his arm warm against mine. I think he's actually watching the movie, but I sure as hell am not. I can't focus on anything but him right now. Until I finally decide to just muster up the courage and do what I'd really like to do. I lean over and kiss him on the cheek. He looks at me with a smile, like he's been waiting for me to do that for the past hour. He kisses the corner of my mouth, and suddenly the laptop is shoved out of the way and he's on top of me, kissing my neck, his hands on my pants—when I sit up.

He's breathing hard. "Are you okay?"

I nod, but I'm nodding too fast.

"Don't worry," he says. "I know what to do."

And he pushes me back to the bed, tugs up my T-shirt, lays kisses all over my skin, kisses that have me catching my breath, until he's got both my pants and my boxers down, and my hands are in his hair, and I don't want him to stop—but he pulls away and starts to pull his own shirt off. He looks more nervous about it now too, and he sits in front of me for a second, until he kisses me. This kiss is slower. I'm on my back again, his leg pressing in between my legs, his mouth on my neck, my chest, my stomach—my skin's burning up.

He sits up, breathing hard. "Are you okay if I'm on top?"

It's a scary thought, but I'm pretty sure I want him to be. I nod and we're still kissing—he pauses and reaches for his nightstand, opens up a drawer, and pulls out a tube of lube. For some reason, the lube is what makes me more embarrassed about any of this. He kisses me again, blocking my view, so I can't really see what he's doing, can only feel his hand slippery and warm, pressing into me, literally inside of me, and it really effing hurts—

"Are you okay?" he asks. He's watching my face closely, intently. I almost want to say no—it hurts, and I'm freaking out. But a part of me doesn't want him to stop either.

I nod. "Yeah. I'm okay."

He buries his face into my neck, his finger moving around,

and I can tell he's trying to be gentle—and the more he moves it around, the more I get used to it, the more it starts to feel good. His mouth is by my ear, breathing against it. He asks if it's okay if he—and he can't really say it out loud, but I know what he means. I nod. Ollie pulls away, seems to swipe a condom out of midair and rolls it on. A wave of nerves washes over me.

He pushes in slowly, and the pain grates. I almost try to push him away.

He pulls back to look at my face. "Does it feel good?"

I try my best to smile and nod so that it doesn't look like I'm grimacing.

He watches me. "It doesn't feel good at all, does it?"

I hesitate, then shake my head, and we're laughing a little together, but I put my hands on his back so he knows I want him to stay. "You can keep going. Maybe it'll start to feel good. Just—you know, move slow."

He keeps going slow, but it never really feels good, though I guess it doesn't hurt as much by the end. We both end up on our backs, just breathing heavy, Ollie's cheeks and chest red. I'm so completely sore that pain springs up my back whenever I move, so I just stay exactly where I am.

He looks at me like he's worried. I take his hand, and he smiles and rolls onto his stomach.

"I can't believe we just did that," I tell him.

"I'm sorry you didn't like it," he says. "I tried to make you feel good."

"I know." I shrug, then immediately regret it, wincing. "It's not your fault. Pretty sure it was going to hurt, no matter what you did." He still looks a little frustrated about it, so I pull him down for a kiss. "I'm willing to bet it's going to feel a lot better next time."

He can't help but grin at that.

Ash has Friendsgiving over at her place every year. She invited Ollie too, but he has to leave for Santa Fe to spend time with his dad. I'm dreading it. I've gotten way too used to spending time with him, before and during and after school, hanging out in his room and going for walks and trying my best not to obsess over him.

"It'll be a week," Ollie says. We're walking back to our neighborhood after school. He won't even have time to hang out—he has to go straight home and grab his backpack and get into the car with his mom so that she can drive him to the airport. "Not a big deal. We'll just eat dinner, stay at home. I know he'll want me to hang out with his girlfriend at some point." Which sounds like a bigger deal.

I hand him my phone. **Is she horrible?**

"Not at all. She's actually really nice." He shrugs. "I just don't want my mother to think I would replace her. That's what she's most afraid of right now, I think."

I get this sudden image: Ollie's dad and his really nice girlfriend. Aiden apologizing, telling Oliver James that he's still in love with him, and Oliver deciding he still loves Aiden too. Ollie deciding to stay in Santa Fe. Suddenly, I'm in a panic that he'll come back and say he and Aiden have decided to give it another shot. Or that this is the last time I'm ever going to see him again.

We stop at the bend in our neighborhood. I turn to face him. "Ollie—are you still talking to Aiden?"

He looks at me with this expression on his face. I can't even blame him. As soon as the words are out of my mouth, I realize how bad it sounds.

He shakes his head. "Where did that come from?"

I shake my head too. Circle a fist around my chest. "Sorry. Just. I mean."

He's waiting, frowning.

"I'm just scared you'll—uh—go back to him, I guess." I rub the back of my neck. He shakes his head in confusion, so I hand him my phone. There's a mix of emotions on his face—impatience, frustration.

Ollie shrugs. "We still talk. But he knows I'm with you now."

I'm being a jealous, insecure asshole. I know that I am.

I point to him, then to my chin and chest, but can't remember the sign for *move back*, so I say aloud, "You'd let me know if you were going to move back to Santa Fe, right?"

Ollie frowns. "I'm not going to."

"But—I mean, you'd still tell me, right? We wouldn't just

stop talking again." Like the way we did when we were kids.

Ollie hesitates, then shakes his head. "No, Bird. I don't think I could ever stop talking to you again."

It shouldn't feel so good to hear that, but it does. Ollie pauses, and I think maybe he wants to hug me goodbye, but then he hesitates, and I'm not sure if what I said actually really upset him—so much he doesn't want to touch me right now—and we just end up standing there awkwardly for a second, because that's the only way I know how to live my life. Ollie signs goodbye, and I wave bye too, before he continues on up the hill and to his house.

I stand on the front steps next to my mom. Things haven't been great between us, and I know it's because I've been avoiding her—because I still haven't apologized for the bullshit I said. *I feel sorry for you.* I mean, who says that to their own mother?

She shouldn't have to demand an apology. She raised me well enough to be able to expect one. But I'm really embarrassed to even bring it up, and whenever I try to tell her that I'm sorry, I can feel the heat getting stuck in my throat, making it hard to force the words out.

We stand there next to each other, not saying anything, and I realize how creepy this is at precisely the last second, when Becca swings into the drive. She gets out of the rental car, slams the door shut, keys jangling. "What is this, the Stepford Wives?"

My mom gives Becca a tight hug. "Missed you, baby girl."

"I missed you too, Mom."

I trail behind awkwardly. Becca turns to me with a grin, ruffles my hair. "Time to shave those sides down again."

We sit together in her old room, which hasn't been turned into a library or a gym or anything my mom jokingly threatened to do when Becca left for college. It's all exactly the way she left it: yellow walls, shelves of trophies and awards and framed photos of friends and family. She's got her clippers buzzing while we sit cross-legged in front of each other. I'm so happy that she's home that I'm not really sure what to say without coming across like someone she'd wish she wasn't related to, so I just stay quiet while she talks about her drive over, this guy who she might be feeling serious about, and (wait for it) how she's been talking to her roommate about me and Oliver James.

"Becca. Seriously. You can't just go around telling people my business."

"Oh, relax, she doesn't give a crap about your high school drama. Keep your head straight."

I turn my head and keep still until she's finished. "There. Looks pretty good."

"Gonna have to trust you on that."

She smacks the back of my neck. I flinch and rub it as she gets up and starts looking through her shelves, maybe checking to see if there are any new additions, or to see if anything's missing.

"How is it being back?" I ask. Maybe hoping I could find a way to start talking about the terrible shit I'd said to Mom.

She shrugs. "A little weird. It's like I went away, got a taste of what it's like to actually be an adult, and then I came back to this house and our mom and . . . now I'm a kid all over again."

"She's still over the deep end, you know—still has that stupid curfew rule, and expects me to text her where I am at every second. I told her about the contest, and she flipped out."

Becca had gotten plenty of updates from me on the contest. "Give her a break, Nate. She's allowed to be human too."

I feel a pang of embarrassment. Suddenly, I don't want to tell her about the fight I had with our mom anymore. I have a feeling Becca would be a little ashamed of me.

She sits down in front of me again and slowly starts to smile. "Aw," she says. "My little brother is growing up."

"Shut up."

"Don't tell me to shut up."

"I just did." Before she can say anything, I quickly add, "Can I ask you something?"

"Of course, little brother."

"Do you think it's better to just—end a relationship before someone gets hurt?"

She frowns at me. "Is this about you and Ollie?"

I shrug. "Yeah."

"Why would one of you get hurt?"

"Because someone always gets hurt."

Becca shakes her head. "You're always so pessimistic, Nate."

"It's not pessimistic to think we might break up. It's realistic. There's a pretty damn big chance that we're not going to spend the rest of our lives together."

"So?" she says, and when I make a face, she says it again, even louder. "So the hell what? You don't need to spend the rest of your life with Ollie to be in love with him now. Yeah, you know what? You probably will do something really shitty and idiotic, and Ollie probably will break up with you for being an asshole."

"Thanks a lot, Becca."

"But even if that happens—that doesn't take away anything that happened before. The present. The fun you'll have, everything you'll learn about yourself. Nothing will take that away. So is it worth it? You're damned right it's worth it."

"You can say that because you're not the one being broken up with."

"Are you just going to refuse to be with anyone for the rest of your life? Stay alone because you're too afraid of heartbreak?"

I have a sudden image of myself: the hermit in the woods, shooting at anyone who comes within twenty feet of his property, because he doesn't want anyone coming too close.

"There's going to be pain," Becca says. "There's always going to be pain and anger and heartbreak and frustration. But there's going to be joy, too."

I have nothing to say. I know that Becca's right. She stands up from her bed and opens her closet, looking through dresses she'd left behind.

"And, for the record, I do think it's going to work out and that you're going to spend the rest of your life with Oliver James."

"I know you know everything. But there's really no way you can know that."

She closes her closet door and walks over with a smile before pinching my arm. "That's true. But I can still hope for the best. It's called optimism, Nate. You should try it sometime."

With Ollie in Santa Fe, I guess this is where a montage would play: eating Friendsgiving with Ash and Gideon and Florence, trying to ignore the awkward tension between Ashley and Gideon (seems they're not nearly as friendly when they're not completely drunk). Shots of me furiously typing away at my laptop with the deadline for the contest inching closer and closer. Becca reading my script aloud and me looking all mortified. Family dinner with laughter, me looking at my calendar and scratching off the days until the contest deadline: ten days now. Just ten days. Usually I'd be freaking out, because it's really hard to get into the flow of writing sometimes, and harder to just keep writing nonstop—but I guess this time, because I've got something to say, the words come a lot easier.

Until I'm done.

End montage scene. First script I've ever finished, and I'm done. I don't really know what to do with myself. What do I do when I've finished writing my first script? This feels epic and anticlimactic all at the same time—like I'd expect for there to be fireworks or a party to burst through my door or something, but I'm just sitting here alone in my room, staring at the words I've written on my screen.

What do I do now?

Well, I guess I know what I'm going to end up doing, ultimately.

I've got to submit this thing.

I sit in front of my laptop, reading the script over from beginning to end a thousand times. I shouldn't get my hopes up. I already know that. There's a chance that I won't get in. That I would've wasted all of these nights, just to be told that my dream is made of shit tacos. That I'll need to find a new dream because I won't be able to do this for the rest of my life.

I can practically hear my sister now.

Right. Optimism, Nate. Optimism.

Rebecca bursts into my room like she could hear me thinking about her. Her total disregard for my privacy used to piss me off when she was still living here, but now it makes me feel nostalgic. I point at my screen.

"It's finished," I tell her.

"What the what?" she says, hopping onto my bed. "Congrats, bro. I'm proud of you."

I can't stop grinning. Stupid, I know.

She twists the screen to her, eyes scanning the final pages— the only words of the script she hadn't read yet since coming for Thanksgiving break. "Ah—nice ending."

"Thanks."

She turns the screen back to me. "Are you going to show Oliver James?"

My smile vanishes. "Why would I do that?"

She gives me a weird look. "Uh—because he's a character in your script?"

"He's not a character."

She stares at me like she can't tell if I'm joking or not.

I roll my eyes. "There's slight inspiration, I guess."

I hadn't planned on showing it to Ollie. I'd spilled open my guts and soul on these pages, and I was ready for the entire world to see it—the entire world but Oliver James. I don't want him to know just how much I love him, just how much I think about him, just how much I want to be with him, because that'll make it all the more painful when everything ends.

"He doesn't need to know that."

She rolls her eyes. "God, you're such a freak."

I feel myself sulking. Being around Becca somehow makes me act like a little kid. "That's not fair. I'm just not comfortable showing him, all right?"

She puts her hands up. "Whatever you say, Nate."

20

BECCA LEAVES WITH A FLURRY OF GOODBYES AND KISSES before she jumps into her rental car and heads back to the airport. The house instantly becomes empty and lonely and quiet again.

My mom stands at the kitchen counter, filing through the mail. She looks up like she's surprised to see me, watches me for a moment more, then smiles and looks back at the mail in her hand.

"I almost thought you were your father for a second," she says.

That breaks my heart a little. "Really?"

"Not your father seven years ago," she says. "More like your father twenty years ago. When he followed me everywhere I went."

I slide onto a stool, watching as she finishes riffling through the mail. "Nothing but bills."

"I'm sorry, Mom."

There. I finally said it. But she doesn't react, so at first I'm afraid I said it too quietly and that I'd have to find the courage to say it again . . . but then she sighs and neatly stacks up the mail in a pile.

"I know." She isn't looking at me anymore, and I feel ashamed of the things I said to her. They've been echoing in my ears, ambushing my brain: *I have to live my own life without worrying about you all of the time—without feeling sorry for you.* Who the fuck says that?

She seems to agree. "You said some pretty hurtful things, Nate."

"I'm sorry." That's all I can think to say—over and over again. But I know it won't be enough. "I didn't mean any of it. I was just angry."

"You want more independence," she says. "I understand that. But you still need to respect me."

I nod, because she's right.

"But I also hear you," she says. "It's true. I've missed your father." She stops, and I'm afraid she's going to start crying, because if she starts crying then I'm going to start crying, and we'll just be sitting here in the kitchen, crying together. She takes a breath. "And with Becca leaving, I've realized that pretty soon I'm going to be alone in this house. It's going to be hard."

I might be crying a little anyway. I wipe my eyes like I don't think my mom will notice. "It's not like I want to leave you here."

"I know. But you're right. You have to get out there and live your life." She smiles and wipes her face. "Look at me, I'm a mess."

"I don't know if I could do it," I tell her.

"What's that?"

I clench my hands together. "Fall in love, just to lose them."

She doesn't answer for a while, and I wonder if I said something insensitive. I usually feel like I can talk about Dad, because I lost him too—but maybe it's different for her. Maybe she's hurting in ways I can't even begin to understand.

She says, "Sometimes the pain is unbearable. I've never felt a grief like this. I mean—seven years later, and we're still crying." I thought we were on the same page of pretending we aren't crying together in the kitchen, but apparently not. She lets out a laugh that surprises me. "But then I think about the days when he was alive, and when we were in love, and I think—it was all worth it. I'd do it all over again if I could." She pats my hand. "I hope you get to experience a love like that."

I've been thinking so much about happy endings—how they don't exist. But looking at my mom now—I'm not even sure it matters. Don't know if they're even really the point.

"Tell me more about this contest," my mom says. "Will

there be RAs present in the dorms?"

"Yes," I say, looking up with some surprise. "And the guest screenwriters come in once a week."

"When do you hear back?"

"By the end of the year."

She cups my cheek like I'm a little kid, and I don't even mind. "Well, I'm sure you'll do fine, Nate."

Florence and I take the bus to downtown—not to do anything, just to stare through windows and talk about bullshit—but the gray clouds that'd been threatening us all morning open up and we're caught in a downpour. We run into the nearest hipster café (brick walls, chalkboards behind the counter, the sweet scent of incense), laughing a little, dripping wet, and ignoring the other customers who give us annoyed looks for breaking the chill vibe.

"You want anything?" I ask her.

"Hot chocolate?" she says, grabbing us seats.

I go up to the register and order, but just as I turn back with our two mugs of hot cocoa and a bonus chocolate croissant, Flo is on her phone.

"Yeah, I'm with him," she says, frowning, looking up at me as I sit back down. She mouths "Gideon" to me. "You know he never looks at his phone."

I check my pockets—must've left it at home again.

"I mean, sure, we're just down by Pike. It's raining like

crazy, though. Okay. All right. Yeah, I'll text it to you." She puts the phone on the sticky wooden tabletop. "Gideon's coming."

I blow on the steaming hot chocolate. "Everything okay?"

"I don't know. He sounded kind of upset."

We don't end up waiting too long. The door bangs open and Gideon, sopping wet, strolls over and wipes red hair plastered to his forehead away from his face. He grabs a chair and sits down.

Flo and I exchange looks. "Hey, Gideon," Florence says.

He sniffs, nods his head at us.

"Uh," I say, "what's going on?"

He takes a breath and leans forward. "Ash isn't talking to me."

Shit. I didn't know what he wanted to talk about, but I sure as hell didn't think this would be it. I clear my throat. "Really?"

"She said she needs space. To think things through or something, I don't know."

Florence sips, stares over the rims of her glasses like she isn't surprised by this news at all. Maybe she isn't. "And how do you feel about that?"

He shrugs. "Pissed, I guess. It's not my fault she's got a crush on me."

I try not to roll my eyes. "Well, it's not like it matters, right? Since you don't feel the same way."

He doesn't say anything. Tears off a piece of Florence's chocolate croissant. "We were still *friends*, though. It's Saturday. We usually play *Overwatch* and order pizza. And there's all this shit that's going on at home, and no offense, but Ash is the only one I can really talk to about it."

"Wait, what?" Florence says. "I take *great* offense to that. What's going on?"

Gideon hesitates. "My mom's sick." He looks up, sees our faces, and quickly adds, "I don't want to talk about it. Not now, anyway."

Flo nods. "Okay. Let us know when you do."

"I will. But Ash—she was just helping me through a lot of that crap, and she won't hang out with me or talk to me, and now I'm stuck on a mission in *Mass Effect* and I need her freaking help."

Flo looks a little alarmed. "Okay. All right. Take a deep breath."

Gideon takes a breath. He rubs his temples. "I mean, Jesus Christ—why'd she have to go and screw everything up? We were good. We were having a good time. And now this crap with crushes and signs and speeches in the middle of lunch. I like her—but I have a reputation."

I frown at him. "What do you mean, a reputation?"

"You know," he says, shifting in his seat a little. "You guys are my friends, but now I've got the soccer team and student council, and the freaking drama club is hounding me to be in their play again this year, and everyone expects me to be this—superstar. And I don't think they'd really consider Ashley a part of that equation."

Florence crosses her arms. "Well, that's an asshole thing to say."

"That's not what *I* think," Gideon tells us. "I think Ash is awesome. We know that she's cool. But everyone expects me to go out with the captain of the cheerleading squad or something. And it's bullshit. I know it's complete bullshit. But it's also the truth."

We all sit in silence for a while.

"I'll tell you what I think," Florence says. "I think it's totally possible and okay to stay friends, if that's what you actually want. But I have a feeling that, if you didn't have your hordes of amazing friends to think about, you'd be going out with Ashley."

He takes another deep breath and glances up at Flo.

"Fuck what other people think," Florence says. "Like who you like. It's not a big deal, all right?"

Gideon doesn't look convinced. "It's not always that easy."

Florence shrugs. "Only if you want it to be complicated."

Gideon blinks a little, and I think Flo's words might actually be sinking in. He glances at me, but I only shrug.

"Don't look at me. Flo's the one who says the smart shit."

Florence nudges me with her shoulder. "Thanks, Bird."

"You're welcome, Lim."

Gideon chews the croissant, eyebrows furrowed with concentration, until he finally nods. "I need to think of a way to say sorry. To really apologize. Don't even bother looking at me, Bird, I'm most definitely not asking you for help."

I put up my hands defensively. "My days of trying to help are over."

Gideon sighs. "I'll think of something. Is it okay if I hang out with you guys for a little while?"

Florence smiles. "Sure, Gideon—as long as we're cool enough to sit with you."

Gideon rolls his eyes, but even he can't help but laugh.

When I get back home, there's a text message waiting on my phone. It's from Ollie. He says he's back, asks if he can come over. I answer yes, and he responds that he'll be here in a few minutes. I sit on the edge of my bed, trying to breathe. I keep thinking about what Becca told me. To show him the script— let him read it. Open myself up, knowing that I could get hurt—taking that risk.

I hear the knocking downstairs, hear my mom greeting Oliver James and laughing between *"Come in, come in!"* and *"How've you been? How's school?"*—making me die a little inside.

I close my eyes, and I swear to God, I've never been this nervous before. I try to do some breathing exercises, until I get dizzy—try to meditate, even though I don't really know how. Why am I scared? Because I've decided to give happiness a shot? To actually enjoy being with Ollie, let myself fall fully and completely in love with him, instead of thinking about how all of this is going to end?

There's a shifting on my bed. I look up to see Oliver James sitting there.

He rubs his fist in a circle around his chest. "I didn't want to interrupt."

"Yeah. Sorry. I was just—"

I get up from the bed, go to the door, and close it before I turn to face him. I lean against it for a second.

"How was Santa Fe?"

He hesitates. Why is he hesitating? His eyes are red—I don't know why I didn't notice it sooner. He signs, asking me to sit down. But I think it'd be better if I stay standing.

"What's going on?"

He starts crying again, totally unashamed like always, just letting the water leak out his eyes and down his face until it drips off his chin. "I have to tell you something."

"Christ, Ollie, what is it?"

"My dad wants me to move back to Santa Fe."

But his dad's wanted him to move back since he got here to Seattle. That's nothing to get upset over, right?

"When I got back, my mom told me she'd spoken with him, and they agreed—agreed it might be better for me to live with him. Until I graduate from high school."

"What?"

He doesn't repeat himself, maybe because he knows I heard him.

"They can't just do that, can they?"

"They're my parents, Nate."

"But that doesn't mean they can just—I don't know, uproot your entire life because they can't figure it out."

He's wiping his eyes, his face, and I don't think he's understood everything I said, but maybe what I have to say isn't what's important right now. "My dad wants me to graduate at the private school I attended there, and my mom thinks that'll help me get into better colleges, and that it'll be better for me to be around my dad right now, since she's so busy with work."

"Bullshit. That's bullshit."

He hesitates. "I kind of think they're right."

I don't think the words fully sink in until he stands up and begins to pace around the room.

"You think that they're right?" I say when he's stopped to face me. "You want to leave?"

"I don't want to go," he says. "You know that."

Suddenly, I'm not too sure.

"But yeah, I think they're right. The school I was going to—it had a really great arts program, and I had a photography teacher that was going to help me with my college applications and had some connections to good schools, and . . . I'm going to move back after the holidays."

A twist of emotions burn through me, and I don't know how to untangle them.

Oliver James is quiet for a full minute. I would know, because I literally sit there and count the seconds. A minute's a long time when you're waiting for your boyfriend to say something that will make everything hurt less.

"We can work something out," Ollie finally says.

"You couldn't work it out with Aiden."

Ollie clenches his jaw, looks away.

I flip my phone around in my hand, type, and pass it to him. **Is it because of Aiden? Did you see him in Santa Fe and decide you want to be with him again?**

Oliver shakes his head. "Don't do that."

I pause, then say, "I'm sorry."

"It's okay," he says, but I don't really believe him.

Oliver sits there for another full minute before he says he's going to go. We weren't really talking anyway. He leaves, and I stay exactly where I am, sitting on the edge of my bed. I'm pissed. Pissed at Ollie, for deciding to go back to New Mexico. Pissed at myself, for giving into my feelings—for letting myself get into this situation in the first place. Pissed I actually thought that if I loved him without hesitation or reservation, we might actually get a happy ending.

Oliver's waiting for me in the courtyard the next day, sitting at our favorite bench, damp from the cool mist that hangs in the air. I sit down beside him, shivering in the cold, and he smiles at me, taking my hand. His hand is warm. He's always warm.

"I was looking up advice on how to make long-distance relationships work," he tells me, "and one of the articles said it helps if we know our goals, so we're already halfway there, since we know we want to spend the summer together, and then college afterward—"

"Ollie," I say, taking my hand away. He stops talking. "I was thinking, and . . ."

His smile starts to fade. He looks at the phone in my hand when I try to give it to him, finally picks it up.

You know, you already tried a long-distance relationship once, and it didn't work out.

He points at me, extends his thumb from his chin while shaking his head, fingerspells A-I-D-E-N.

"Right, I know I'm not—but . . ."

Long-distance relationships are hard.

"We can make it work."

What if we meet someone else we like? It's probably better to just end it now, right?

He's shaking his head slowly, brows pinched together in confusion.

I hand the phone back to him. **I don't want to wait for you.**

He stands up from the bench before he's even read the entire message, starts walking away—then turns back to me and points at me, spins his finger in a circle, makes Cs and moves his hands back and forth, points downward. "You always—freak out when things aren't going smoothly, aren't going your way. They're not always going to go your way, Nate."

"Right. Yeah, well, I guess I just don't see the point in keeping this going."

"What? What'd you say?" He snatches my phone from me when I'm done typing, shakes his head as he pushes it back at me. "The point is that we like each other, and we can make this work."

"I don't want to make it work." I shrug. I like you—but not enough to stress out over something like this. His eyes flick away from my phone's screen and he stares at me, motionless. I hesitate, type, and hold up the phone for him to read again. This was just for fun, right? We were just messing around.

I feel like I'm boring a hole into my own chest, but I keep my expression blank. Ollie turns on his heel and moves so quickly that he disappears behind the front doors of the school before I can even think of anything else to say. I sit there on the bench, the bottoms of my jeans getting damp, even after the bell rings and everyone out in the courtyard begins to file inside. My phone buzzes, and I have a text from Ollie.

You're right. We should just end it now.

21

OLLIE ISN'T WAITING FOR ME AT THE CORNER TO WALK TO
school the next morning, and he isn't in the courtyard. I don't
see him in the hallways or in the one class we have together in
the morning. Just because we aren't boyfriend and boyfriend
anymore doesn't mean I can't be worried about him. I text
him, asking if he's all right, but he doesn't respond.

Maybe things for me and Ollie won't be the same as for
me and Flo. Maybe he'll never speak to me again, just like
when we were kids—except this time, I'm the one that ran
away. The thought alone makes my chest hurt, but maybe it's
for the best—a clean break between us, instead of trying to
stay friends, knowing that I'm in love with him.

When I get to the greenhouse, he isn't there either—but

something else grabs my attention: Ashley is holding Gideon's hand on top of the table.

They barely glance up at me before they turn right back to each other—talking low under their voices, about what I don't know, Gideon turning Ashley's palm over in his hand, Ashley pecking his cheek.

I slide onto the bench beside Flo and whisper to her, "When the hell did that happen?"

She leans closer to me. "According to Ashley, Gideon went over to her place last night and said it took him a while to figure out, but he wants to be together. So they're official now." She makes a face as we watch them. "It's actually a little grossly sweet."

Grossly sweet might be an understatement—but I'm happy for them too, especially after trying to help Ashley out and failing. But I can't ignore that the happiness is tinged a little with something else also—something a little ugly. I feel bad. This isn't about me and Ollie. This is about Gideon and Ashley.

"Congratulations," I say to them, and they both look up with these bright, glowing smiles.

"Thanks," Ashley says. "Wouldn't have happened without you, I guess."

Gideon shrugs. "It could've happened without him."

Ashley squints at him. "I mean, probably, but not really."

They start bicker-banter-flirting. I'm pretty sure they'll

keep it up for the entire lunch period if no one stops them.

I clear my throat. "Where's Ollie? I haven't seen him all morning."

"He's home sick," Florence says, glancing up at me from the sketch in her notebook. "He texted me last period."

I look down at the ground, wondering if he texted her anything else. From the way Flo watches me, I think he might have. Gideon says something to make Ashley let out a laugh, and the two of them look so incredibly happy, and they'll have the rest of the year and summer vacation and all of next year together, before they'll probably go off to the same college together and get married and tell everyone they meet that they're high school sweethearts with the cutest story about how Ashley made an idiot of herself by announcing to the whole school that she had a crush on Gideon.

I get to my feet, ignore Flo when she asks where I'm going, walk out of the greenhouse into the fresh winter air. I hear footsteps behind me. Florence jogs a little to catch up.

"You okay?" she says, a little breathless, as she stuffs her hands into her pockets.

"I guess Ollie told you."

"He texted me last night," she admits. She stops in front of me so that I have to stop walking and look her in eye. "I'm really sorry, Bird."

I shake my head. "It's all right. I didn't really think it was going to work out anyway."

264

She frowns. "I did. I was so sure it would work out." She pauses. "And I still think it can."

"How? How could this work?"

She ignores my annoyed tone. "You're the one who decided a long-distance relationship meant a bad ending."

"It was for him and Aiden."

"You're not Aiden," Florence says without missing a beat. "It could be different for you and Ollie, but you'll never know if you don't give it a chance."

"I already gave it a chance," I say, a little more loudly than necessary. "I already tried it, already tried being with him, and it failed. Simple as that. And I shouldn't really be surprised."

"What does that mean?"

It means there aren't any happy endings, not in real life, and it doesn't make any sense to try to force one to happen. "I have homework for physics," I tell her. "I'll talk to you later, all right?"

I start walking, and I can feel Flo's gaze still on me as I walk through the school's front doors.

The second week in December rolls around. Ollie comes back to school, looking paler than usual with bags under his eyes, like he hasn't been getting very much sleep. I did that to him. I know I did. But I can't bring myself to talk to him about it, and he doesn't have anything to say to me either. So we end up not speaking, just giving each other stupid and awkward waves and head nods whenever we pass each other in the hallways, and, in the greenhouse, we stay on opposite ends of the bench with Ashley and Gideon sitting in between us.

"Did something happen between you and Oliver James?" Ashley whispers to me as Ollie, Gideon, and Flo chat about their last class, Florence handing Ollie her phone every now and then.

"No, not really."

"It's just that . . . you two seem really distant recently."

I shrug. "Well, we broke up."

Her eyes almost bug out of her head. Her mouth drops open. "What?" she says, loudly enough that Gideon and Flo swing their heads to look at us, and Ollie follows suit. "Why?"

I'm not sure I should be saying any of this. "I mean. Ollie's moving back to Santa Fe."

Ashley, Gideon, and Florence are quiet for a long while, until finally Gideon asks, "When?"

I glance at Ollie. It's not really my place to tell them any of this. "After winter break, I think."

"But that's only in a few weeks," Ashley says, turning to Oliver James.

From the way Ollie's face falls, I can tell he'd meant to keep this a secret for as long as possible. He shrugs. "I just didn't want the last few weeks to be sad."

"It would've been even worse if we didn't know. What if we didn't have a chance to say goodbye?"

"It was his decision not to say it, all right?" I tell Ashley.

She looks surprised, her mouth turning into the Ashley Perkins "O" while she glances between us. Ollie's watching me. The bell rings, and I get up from the bench immediately and head straight for class.

I get home, and for once I wish it were raining. It might be a little unoriginal, but rain would match my mood—make me feel a little better, to see that the weather is crappy too. I stomp the ice off on the doormat and step inside, tugging off my boots. My mom's in the kitchen, drinking some steaming peppermint tea.

"Smells good," I tell her.

"Do you want some?"

I open the fridge. "No thanks."

"Nate?"

I turn around. She's holding up an envelope. It has *Emerging Creatives* at the top of its New York City address. I almost drop the milk bottle I'm holding.

"It's barely been three weeks."

"They must work quickly." She's smiling a little, but my mom looks just as nervous as I do. "Well? Don't just stand there."

I swallow, put the milk back, close the fridge door. She hands me the envelope, and I tear it open. I fumble with the paper, somehow unable to get the letter itself straight, and have to turn it over before I begin reading it aloud:

"'Dear Nathan Bird. We regret to inform you . . .'"

My eyes start to skim the words. Over the top of the paper, I see my mom's face fall a little. I slide into one of the stools and put the letter on the counter. "It was a long shot anyway."

My mom puts a hand on my arm. "There'll be other programs. Like I told you—you don't need this one to be a writer."

"Yeah. That's true." And maybe it's for the best, too. Oliver James definitely would've gotten in, and shit's been so awkward and tense between us . . . I wouldn't want to take that all the way from Seattle to New York. He deserves a Nathan Bird–free summer where he really gets to work on his art.

I shake my head. "Besides, I got to finish my first script because of the application," I say, then ignore the pang in my chest. Ollie had originally been the one to tell me that was at least one reason to apply.

My mom takes the letter to read it herself, then frowns and puts down the mug with a clatter on the counter. "Wait," she says, holding the letter up. "This says that you didn't win the contest because of the level of competitive applications—but that you're invited to the program itself, to take screenwriting classes."

"Yeah," I say, "but that's mostly for students that already live in New York. I'd have to find a place to stay, not to mention tuition. It'd be too expensive."

"So you decided all on your own that you're not going to

be able to afford to go? Are you the one actually paying any bills?"

I frown at her. "But you said—you're the one that said—"

She takes a deep breath, reading over the letter again. "It's expensive," she says, nodding her agreement. She glances up at me. "But I know this is something you really want. I'll make it work."

I can feel my mouth drop open, and I almost throw myself off the stool to give her a hug. "Are you serious?"

"Yes," she says, "but I have a few conditions: keep up your grades. Only As and Bs for the rest of the year."

"I can do that."

"And you'll need to get a job to help," she says.

"Done. Maybe Sparrow and Nightingale is looking for a barista."

She starts to smile. "Well, then," she says, "congratulations, Emerging Creative."

22

THE LAST DAY OF SCHOOL BEFORE WINTER BREAK ENDS with a flurry of goodbyes. Florence and her dad are going to Los Angeles for the holiday, and Ashley and Gideon will be spending Hanukkah and Christmas together with their families. When we're in the greenhouse for lunch, Ash asks Oliver James what he plans to do for the holiday break, and he tells her that he's going to spend the next couple of weeks focusing on packing. He doesn't look at me when he says it. I want to ask him if he won the Emerging Creatives contest. If there's a chance we really could see each other in New York this summer. But he doesn't look at me in the hallways, or as he passes by in the courtyard on the way home either. I know he doesn't want to speak to me right now. Maybe he'll never speak to me again.

* * *

Becca flies in from Chicago a week before Christmas, bundled up in an oversized coat and a giant infinity scarf. I laugh when she steps out of her rental car in the driveway and follows me into the house.

"You look like you're prepared to visit Antarctica."

She begins to unravel her scarf the second she steps into the foyer, shrugs off the coat. "It was freezing in Chicago. Why did I choose Chicago?"

Mom's waiting in the living room. She wraps Becca in a hug and kisses her cheek. Becca rolls her eyes with a grin as she wipes her face. "You always act like I'm ten," she says.

"It doesn't matter how old either of you get," she says, pointing at both of us. "You'll always be my babies."

"Oh God," Becca says. "Let's get out of here before she breaks into song."

Mom laughs, hopping onto the couch. "Come down in a few minutes after you're settled. We'll eat dinner."

Rebecca follows me up the stairs and, after a quick stop in her bedroom where she puts down her bags, we walk down the hall and into my own room.

"Are you going to shave my sides for me again?" I ask.

She considers it, then ruffles my hair. "Nah. I like it growing out on you."

She plops down on the edge of my bed. "Good to see your room hasn't changed."

"It's only been a month. It wouldn't change that drastically."

She sits quietly, waiting for me to speak. Maybe she can tell something's on my mind. But I don't really want to talk about Oliver James. Not right now. I've already told her everything that happened with Ollie. Even admitted what I said, as harsh as it all was—as ashamed of myself as I am. Becca listened. Didn't have any judgment. It's more than I could've asked for.

I turn around from my VHS collection. *Pulp Fiction*, *The Big Lebowski*, *10 Things I Hate About You*: classics. "You know, I got into that summer program for screenwriting in New York. Emerging Creatives."

"Yeah, the one you were writing the script for over Thanksgiving break."

"Mom's letting me go."

Surprise flits across her face. "Really? That's great. That's so great."

She gets up, crosses the room, gives me a hug before she pulls on one of my curls. "That'll be good to put in college applications. My brother, the screenwriter." She grins. "You need to remember me when you get an Oscar."

I laugh. "You'll probably storm the stage and snatch the trophy away."

Her smile starts to fade. "Nate," she says. "What's going on with you and Ollie?"

I sigh, sit down on the side of my bed. "He's moving back to New Mexico, and long-distance relationships never really work, and—I don't know, it's a situation that's just not going to end well. I don't really want to put either of us through that."

"Sounds to me like you're making up a lot of it in your head before it's even happened."

"What?"

"You're assuming the future, but you don't actually know how anything's going to work out. It's a shame you're ending things with him because you're afraid."

I watch her for a second and look at the ground, blinking fast. "I—uh—just think about Dad a lot, I guess, and I wonder what it'd be like for Mom right now if he were still alive."

"I know," she says. "But you can't let Dad's death define every relationship you have from now on. He wouldn't want you to be afraid to let yourself love other people."

She's right. I know she's right. I close my eyes, wipe them with my palms. "I fucked up. I want to be with him."

"Then be with him."

"I don't think he wants to be with me. I fucked up big-time, Becks."

"Then apologize."

"It's not that easy. I don't think he's going to forgive me. There's a cap on assholery, you know?"

She smirks, shaking her head. "It has to be worth a shot. You don't know what he's going to say or do."

I sigh, lean back on my elbows. "I'd have to really do something to make it up to him."

She grins. "I'm sure you can think of something."

"He could throw it all in my face, and he'd have every right to do it."

"Well, you'll never know until you try, right?"

Mom tries to cook, but that's never been her forte—even when we were kids, Dad was always the one in the kitchen—so after burning the roast pork, she calls for three pizzas and we join her in the living room, eating from our own personal boxes, talking through the *Friends* marathon, not really about much—the script I wrote that got me a place at the Emerging Creatives program, Becca's psychology classes and how she's thinking of becoming a therapist (which I think she'd be excellent at, to be honest), Mom's copyediting job and how she's starting to think about writing a book herself.

"I guess you inspired me, Nate," she says with a glance over her shoulder, and that's about the nicest thing anyone's ever told me.

"Oh, I love this episode," Becca says. "It's 'The Last One.'"

I glance at the screen. I hadn't really been watching. "I don't think I've seen it."

Both Becca and Mom turn to look at me. They look eerily alike in their appalled shock.

"What do you mean, you've never seen 'The Last One'?" Becca asks.

I glance away from them. "I mean I've never seen 'The Last One.'"

"Mom watches *Friends* all of the time, and you've never seen 'The Last One'?"

"Okay, can we stop saying 'The Last One,' please?"

Mom sits up from her spot on the floor and gets comfortable on the couch. "It's one of my favorites. You have to see it."

So we do. I know enough about the characters to understand who's who and what's going on. Mom and Becca start to argue whether I'm more like Ross or Monica, and Mom says I'm more like Monica because I'm a bit neurotic, and Becca says I'm more like Ross because I'm a dweeb, and I try to ignore them as Ross and Rachel have a beautiful scene together before they sleep together (which isn't embarrassing to watch with my mom and my sister *at all*), and she tells him that this is the perfect way to say goodbye. Typical heartbreak.

"Oh, my favorite part is coming up," Becca says, and cracks up as the entire plane freaks out over the left phalange.

"And my favorite part is coming up," my mom says, as Ross declares his love for Rachel, but is rejected as she gets back on the plane.

We sit quietly when he returns home, listens to a voice message—hears Rachel realize that she loves Ross too. She struggles to get off the plane, and Ross freaks out over whether she made it off or not, until Mom and Becca say at the same time as Rachel, standing in the doorway, "*I got off the plane.*"

They're both crying (and, fine, I might be a little too), and it's one of the sappiest, sweetest scenes I've ever watched, and I realize that there isn't anything wrong with sappy, sweet scenes—they're just a celebration of life and joy and love, feelings I'm happy I got to experience. . . .

Suddenly, I know exactly what I have to do.

I jump to my feet, ignore Becca when she asks me what I'm doing. I race into my room, rummage through the stacks of papers I have printed on my desk, until I find a copy of the application I'd mailed (just in case something happened to the first set)—pull out the script before I run back down the stairs again, almost tripping when I hit the bottom. *This will work. This has to work.*

Both Mom and Becca are twisted in their seats, watching me like I've lost my mind—and yeah, maybe I have.

"Wait—where're you going?" Becca calls out to me. "You haven't seen the ending yet."

I grab my coat, throw my scarf around my neck. "I'll be right back."

"But—" Mom says, and I know what she's about to say. It's eight o'clock, an hour after curfew. But she meets my eyes, and I can tell she gets it—understands this is important to me . . . and maybe she's starting to see she's going to have to let go of me eventually, too. She nods. "Be back in exactly one hour, or I'm calling the police."

"Okay, got it," I say, throwing open the front door. "I'll be back soon."

This should be quick. All I have to do is go up the hill. I run, dodging the roots that break up the sidewalk, and get to the front door before I begin to knock. Donna Noble starts to bark, and the door swings open. Ollie's mom stands in front of me.

"Nate," she says, stepping outside, wiping her hands on a towel like she'd just been doing the dishes. "It's nice to see you." She pulls me into a hug, but it's a little stiff. Her son probably told her everything that happened—everything I said. "Are you here to see Oliver James?"

I nod, breathless from running up the hill.

She glances at the papers in my hands. "I'm sorry, but he isn't here. He said he was going out for a walk about an hour ago."

I look at the ground, still breathing heavy. I hadn't factored this into my plan.

"You're welcome to come inside and wait for him to come back."

I look up at her, suddenly struck. "No—no, I think I know where he might've gone."

She nods. "Okay. Well, it was nice to see you."

"Nice to see you too, Mrs. Hernández," I say over my shoulder, before I run down the street and toward the lake.

It starts to snow a little—the first time it's snowed all year—and I know it's setting the perfect scene: a still lake, flurries of crystals shining through the air, Ollie's red cheeks. I keep running, until finally I'm there, shoes crunching along the shore, overheated despite the cold, completely out of breath. I see the boulder, and I see him, standing at the water and staring out at it. I don't want to scare him by sneaking up on him, so I walk slowly, wave my hands until he sees me in the corner of his eye.

Oliver James turns to me, surprised. "What're you doing here?"

"I—" How do I explain that I was watching *Friends*, and it made me realize that I couldn't just lose him, not without trying, not without showing how much I love him? It sounds ridiculous. But he's waiting for me to say something, watching me with an expression that's turning to anger, like he's remembering everything that I told him before.

I take a deep breath. "You'd asked to read my script."

He looks at the papers in my hands, looks back up at me.

"I wanted to give it to you. Before you left."

He squints at me. "Nate, what's going on?"

"Please," I say. I step forward, holding the pages out. "Just read it."

He shakes his head. "I don't want to."

Air catches in my throat. I hadn't factored this into my plan either. I keep holding the papers up, unsure of what to do or say.

"You treated me like complete shit, Nate," he says, his voice getting louder, angrier.

I look at the ground. "I know. I'm sorry."

"You treated me like I meant nothing to you."

"I—I explain everything in the script."

I think he hasn't understood me—or that he's ignoring me—but then he swallows, takes the pages from my hand, and for a second I think he's going to throw it into the lake, and maybe he really is about to—but then he rolls it up and puts it into his coat pocket. "I'll read it."

"Before you leave."

"I said I'll read it."

He tugs on his ear, shakes his head again, and starts walking. I start to follow, but he stops. "I'd like to walk back by myself."

His words take me by surprise. I've never seen Oliver James this angry. I nod, watch him leave—lean against the boulder and stay there a good ten minutes.

This script has to work. Even if he doesn't want me anymore—even if he can't forgive me for the things I said—it has to show him how much I care about him. That's all that I need.

23

CHRISTMAS COMES AND GOES, AND IT'S NICE TO SPEND SO much time with Becca and our mom—I don't think we've ever hung out this much before, not since Dad passed away. Maybe Becca being off at college and everything Mom and I have been through this year has created a new togetherness for us. But even while we're watching TV or movies or playing board games, I know they can tell I'm distracted. I keep checking my phone, hoping to see a text message from Oliver James saying that he wants to talk, but it never comes.

Florence flies back to Seattle from Los Angeles, so I go to her house, letting Tobey Maguire have his usual fun before she picks him up and gives me a one-armed hug. "It feels like I haven't seen you in months."

"I know."

We go to her bedroom, and once upon a time it would've been physically painful to be here with her, unable to touch her or kiss her or say how much I love her, but now it feels fine. Maybe I've gotten used to the way things are between us now. I do still love her, and I hope I always will—but it's a comfortable sort of love now.

I think of telling her about the script and Oliver, how I'm hoping he'll read it so that he'll know how I feel—but sitting there in her room with Ethel and Tobey Maguire, I realize I just want to be with her, in this moment. She ends up drawing a portrait of me, and it's pretty effing good, and she tells me about the art schools she wants to apply to. Colleges all over the country. She'll probably end up thousands of miles away from me—but that doesn't worry me as much. I know I'll always be there for Flo, and she'll always be there for me.

She smiles at me from her desk. "We had a pretty good run, didn't we, Bird?"

I can't help but grin. "Yeah. We did."

"Nathan Bird and Florence Lim. I don't think there's a more iconic pair of best friends."

I might have to agree with that, too.

I wait for Oliver to text me, but he never does, and as the days pass, I'm starting to figure out that he never will. Becca has to fly back to Chicago, which honestly sucks. We've always been pretty close, but somehow, these holidays just brought us closer than we'd ever been before. Maybe we're both growing up a little, so it's easier to talk about the things that really matter.

The night she drives off to the airport, my mom and I end up sitting together comfortably in the living room. I still can't believe how crappy I've been to her these past few months, and every now and then, the shame and embarrassment rolls into me again. My mom's made it clear that she wasn't happy with the way I treated her, but she's also made it clear that she loves me and forgives me. I know that I'm lucky to have a mom like her.

"Are you going to be all right when I leave for college?" I ask.

"Of course," she says. "I'll just have to keep myself busy. My Tinder profile is helping."

I hide my face in my hands. "Oh God, Mom."

She laughs. "Seriously, Nate, I don't want you to worry about that. All right? I want you to go out there and live your life."

"All right." I wrinkle my nose. "How's the dating going?"

She gives me a look. "Do you really want to know?"

I shake my head. "Not at all."

She tugs on one of my curls. "If it gets serious with anyone, I'll tell you—but until then, you don't have to worry about it. Sound good?"

I nod. "Yeah. Sounds good."

* * *

It's the night before Ollie leaves Seattle for Santa Fe, and he never texted me—never said he even read the script. It was a solid effort, but I know it's too late now. But I don't want to be sad about that. I mean, I will be—for a few weeks or months or years, or maybe even for the rest of my life, I'll think back on this moment, the time when I lost Oliver James Hernández for good—but I think I'll find a way to be happy too. I have the feeling that it's not always going to work out—that I'll have my heart broken a few more times in my life. Sitting here, right now with my mom, I realize that's all right. Maybe the ending isn't even really the point. Just as long as there was a *happy* somewhere along the way.

There's a knock on the door. My mom raises an eyebrow, glancing away from the TV. "Would you get the door, Nate?"

My heart starts to hammer against my chest, but I tell my heart to calm the fuck down, because there's no point in getting overexcited. There's a chance that it's him . . . but there's a bigger chance that it isn't. I shrug, get to my feet, cross to the foyer, open the door.

Ollie's standing there.

I have a distinct memory of me, sitting beside him in his bedroom, putting my hand on top of his. He stands, waits, script in his hand. I step outside and close the door behind me.

He holds it up. "I read it."

I take the script back. It's hard to look at him, but I force myself to.

He gestures at the papers in my hand. "Did you really

mean everything you wrote?"

I nod. "Yeah."

"Everything about being sorry and—afraid . . ."

"I wrote it—I don't know, based on how I feel about you."

He closes his eyes for a second, takes a deep breath, before he opens his eyes again. "You really hurt me, Nate."

"I know. I'm sorry."

"But—I guess I can understand. Not that you'd say the shit you said," he adds, "but why you did it. I'm afraid too. I have no idea how this is going to end. Aiden and I didn't work out, and I've been really afraid of losing you again."

"That's why this is killing me. I fucked up."

"Wait. Slow down," he says.

I pull out my phone, hand it to him. **I don't want this to be how everything ends for us.**

He's watching me carefully. "It doesn't have to."

I wait, scared to even breathe—like the air will blow away any chance I have with him.

"It'll take a lot of work," he says. "From both of us."

I nod. "Yeah."

"And instead of freaking out," he says, stepping closer, "you should just talk to me and explain how you're feeling. If you're scared or frustrated."

"Yeah."

"Or—I don't know—write out a scene if you can't figure out how to say it."

I laugh a little. "Yeah."

He touches my fingers with his. "You'll have to text and video chat with me every day."

I can't help but smile. "That won't be a problem."

He takes my hand, turns it over to look at my palm before he puts his own hand on top of mine, intertwining our fingers. My heart might just implode, but I don't want to let myself get hopeful—not until I hear him actually say the words.

Ollie looks at me. "So—then—I guess we can try this again."

I feel like I could cry and laugh and go streaking through the neighborhood all at once. "Is it all right if I hug you?"

He nods, so I wrap my arms around him, his head nestled beneath my chin, and he feels so good against my body, his arms around my back. I know this isn't going to be easy—but for Oliver James Hernández, I'll take any time I have with him: the hard, the easy, the good, the bad. As long as I have him.

Ollie takes me down to Green Lake. On the walk over, he tells me that he got into the Emerging Creatives program, and I tell him that I got in too—we'll be able to spend the summer together in New York, just like we'd planned. And after the summer, it'll only be one more year before we can decide what we want to do—if we'll be together in college. One year isn't so long, when you think about it.

The lake's got melting ice crunching on the shore. We're both shivering, and coming here probably wasn't the best idea, but I guess neither of us really cares about how cold it is. He wraps his arms around my waist and I pull him closer, and we just stand there for a while, shaking every time the breeze blows a little too hard.

He pulls away from me. "This was a lot, right?"

I laugh. "Pretty much."

"To go back and forth and end up here—I wasn't so sure it'd work out, you know?"

I nod. His head nestled beneath my chin, I pull out my phone and type, arms still around his back, and pull away so that he can read. **I never really thought this would happen. I guess I just have a hard time believing in happy endings.**

"Wait, what? What do you mean, you don't believe in happy endings?"

"I mean—I don't know." **This is the kind of thing that happens in movies. It doesn't happen in real life.**

Ollie tilts his head, watching me. "Of course it happens in real life. It happens all the time." He's smiling, back to looking at my mouth. "What else are those movies supposed to be based on, if happy endings don't actually exist?"

I don't have an answer for him, so I have to agree. I can't help but lean in a little to kiss him and pull him closer.

I'm realizing it doesn't really matter if we have a happy ending or not. We're happy right now. That's the important part, right?

ACKNOWLEDGMENTS

I'm an incredibly lucky person to be surrounded by the amazing, passionate people who have helped me to put *This Is Kind of an Epic Love Story* out into the world:

Beth Phelan, agent extraordinaire, who—at least at one point—I'm pretty sure believed in this book more than I did.

Alessandra Balzer, powerhouse editor, who got the book from the beginning, understood everything I wanted to accomplish, and helped me reach those goals and more.

The entire HarperCollins team who brought this book into existence, including Kelsey Murphy, Bess Braswell, Ebony LaDelle, Andrea Pappenheimer, Kathy Faber, Kerry Moynagh, Paul Crichton, Bethany Reis, Michelle Cunningham, Alison

Donalty, Nathan Burton, Patty Rosati, Molly Motch, and Kristen Eckhardt.

Early readers Shannon Rogers, Jennifer Poe, and Ashley Woodfolk—I probably wouldn't have kept writing this without your initial excitement for Nate, Flo, and Ollie!

My infinite thanks for the insight and patience of Becca Wasilewski.

My mom, Barbara Callwood, who has always been such a tireless advocate of my writing, and who I always look to for support when I inevitably begin to question myself.

And, finally, I'm lucky for all the queer people of color who exist in the world, who inspire me and make me feel a little less alone. We're beautiful, we're magical, and we deserve epic love stories, too.